LOVE YOU TRULY

Anjali Rai

Om Books International

First published in 2021 by

Om Books International

Corporate & Editorial Office
A-12, Sector 64, Noida 201 301
Uttar Pradesh, India
Phone: +91 120 477 4100
Email: editorial@ombooks.com
Website: www.ombooksinternational.com

Sales Office
107, Ansari Road, Darya Ganj,
New Delhi 110 002, India
Phone: +91 11 4000 9000
Fax: +91 11 2327 8091
Email: sales@ombooks.com
Website: www.ombooks.com

Disclaimer: This is a work of fiction. Names, characters, businesses, places, events and incidents are either the products of the author's imagination or used in a fictitious manner. Any resemblance to actual persons, living or dead, or actual events is purely coincidental.

ISBN: 978-93-53764-06-7

Printed in India

10 9 8 7 6 5 4 3 2 1

Contents

1

Moving On

Lalsa was returning to Delhi from Mussoorie, a place that had been her home for the last nine years. She was leaving behind her school and hostel where she had completed her primary and secondary education. The car that was taking her back home was moving along the lush green hills of Mussoorie, while driving down. Last night's celebrations had gone on till late and Lalsa was very exhausted. Sleepily, she slouched on the car seat, closed her eyes and dozed off.

Halfway through their journey to Delhi, the driver stopped the car. Lalsa stepped out, grabbed a sandwich and a coffee which made her feel fresh again. She took out her mobile phone and scrolled through last night's photographs of the party with her friends. Her friends belonged to different cities and each one of them held a very special place in Lalsa's heart. Reminiscing about her school days, she saw her group photo from third standard, when she had been admitted to her school in Mussoorie, and her childhood emerged from the mists of time.

Lalsa as a little baby, was adorable and had grown up into a beautiful girl with large, brown expressive eyes and soft features. Her long, silky hair won the hearts of everyone around her. Born into a Punjabi family, she was a single child brought up by a businessman father and a mother who was Lalsa's shadow. She was never left alone as her mother was possessive about her beautiful daughter and also feared that her daughter's beauty might attract unwanted attention and lecherous people.

Lalsa's father had to go out of station very often for his business commitments but he compensated for his absence by showering extra affection, gifts and large sums of money on both mother and daughter during his short stays at home. Her father never wanted his daughter to be away from him. But her mother was obsessed by the way one of Lalsa's cousins had been groomed into a fine lady by a school in Mussoorie. So she had promised herself that if she ever had a daughter, she would be sent to the same school.

Lalsa distinctly remembered the day when her mother and father had taken her to Mussoorie for admission to Saint Mary Girls' Convent. On their way, she had sat in the back seat of the car between her parents. Her father had kissed her little hand again and again with a heavy heart at the thought of parting with his little girl.

Lalsa thoroughly enjoyed her hostel life and grew up into a feisty and assertive girl. She was never scared of anybody and sometimes was even contemptuous of the people who misbehaved with her. She was popular among the girls and shot fame because of a face-off with one of her teachers. There were two categories of teachers in their school–the nuns whom they called 'Sisters' wore white clothes and 'Misses' who wore short tight skirts with smart blazers. Her maths teacher, Miss Maggie was a portly lady who loved to wear pencil-heeled shoes with her short skirt. One day, while writing on the blackboard, she lost her balance and stumbled badly. Lalsa started sniggering along with the other students of the class. Listening to the noise, Miss Maggie got exasperated and turned back furiously. She saw Lalsa sitting on the front bench with a mischievous smile on her face.

She asked her angrily, "Stand up and tell me why you are laughing?"

"Miss...!" Lalsa burst into an exuberant laugh without completing the sentence.

The teacher couldn't control her anger. She gave Lalsa a tight slap on her cheek.

Lalsa didn't expect such an outburst from her teacher. She was stunned for a moment but immediately regained her senses and said, "How can you slap me, Miss? You can't hurt me physically. I shall complain to the principal." Before the teacher could utter a word, she had left the classroom and rushed to the principal. The principal intervened and the teacher had to apologise for raising her hand on Lalsa. This incident established Lalsa as a star student of the school. Everybody discussed and appreciated her courage to challenge the authority and the behaviour of her teacher.

Over time, Lalsa developed a close friendship with Sanya who was a quiet girl with a lot of patience. Although they were of the same age, Lalsa, somehow, felt more responsible towards her, like an older sister and whenever Lalsa became aggressive, Sanya calmed her down with her rational persuasion. They may have been complete opposites but complemented each other beautifully. Sanya and Lalsa seemed to live up to the adage that 'opposites attract'.

The rules of the school were very strict. The inmates grew up under the strict and vigilant supervision of the nuns who taught them discipline, hard work and skills like embroidery, cooking, dancing, singing and spoken English along with table manners to transform them into fine ladies. They were not allowed to go out of the school without a request letter from their parents. The unquestioned wisdom behind was to ensure the safety and morality of the girls.

One day, one of their hostel mates, Shuchi, had her cousin Rajan visiting her. He was a thirty-year old married man from Dehradun and had always been very fond of Shuchi. He had come especially from Dehradun to meet her. He wanted to take her out for a few hours, but didn't have a request letter from her parents. In order to take Shuchi out, he had forged the parents' letter and taken Shuchi out for lunch.

In the evening, when Shuchi returned to the hostel, she was very upset. She refused to have dinner, saying that she wasn't well. When Lalsa and Sanya came back after having dinner, they saw her crying into her pillow. They realised that all was not well with her. Lalsa gently persuaded Shuchi to talk about whatever was troubling her.

Shuchi confided in her friends about what had transpired. She told them that her cousin, Rajan, had taken her out for lunch to the hotel where he was staying and had ordered food in his room. While having lunch Shuchi sensed that his mind was preoccupied with something else. He was hardly paying attention to her conversation nor was he eating anything. Shuchi realised that he seemed very restless and kept changing his posture while sitting on the chair in front of her; his face and ears had also turned red. Observing his strange behaviour, Shuchi too became uncomfortable. She finished lunch and got up to leave.

"Now, drop me back as I have some urgent work to finish," Shuchi said politely.

Rajan was taken aback by her reaction. He immediately stood up, held her hand and said, "Oh dear, why do you want to go so soon? I like you so much and have especially come to meet you. We seldom get a chance to be alone."

"I want to go back," Shuchi insisted firmly this time.

"Come on dear, spend some time with me!" Rajan said and tried to draw her close to his chest.

"Rajan *bhaiya,* please let go of me!" Shuchi said sternly and loudly and at the same time fearfully and angrily.

"Don't be so conservative. Nobody would ever come to know about it. Let's enjoy!" Rajan dragged her to the bed.

Shuchi fell down on the bed. By then she was very scared.

"Leave me! Let me go!" Shuchi had started shouting.

She picked up the phone lying the bedside and said, "I will call the police."

Rajan had probably not expected such a strong reaction from her. He was taken aback by his cousin's resistance and threats.

His face turned pale. "I think you are misunderstanding me. If you want to go, I will drop you right now." He said with embarrassment.

"No thanks, I will go on my own!" Shuchi said and rushed out of the room.

The incident had really shocked her. She revisited those moments several times and was convinced that had she not managed the situation assertively, a disaster could have happened.

On hearing Shuchi's account, Lalsa became extremely agitated and advised her to call her parents and tell them the truth there and then. But Sanya opined not to disturb her parents at night. She advised Shuchi to try to sleep and talk to her parents in the morning in a calm frame of mind. Shuchi agreed to Sanya's advice and felt better after she had shared her experience with both of them.

Lalsa recalled how her mother had always been very vigilant about her safety. She always warned her not to touch or let her cousins or uncles touch her. She remembered the day when she was seven years old and her uncle had bought a doll for her. Happily, she had sat in her uncle's lap and kissed him many times on his cheeks to express her gratitude. That same day, her mother had cautioned her, to never kiss or sleep with any male member of the family because her innocent trust could be abused. Lalsa did not understand this completely at that point of time, but had always heeded her mother's warning.

Reminiscences of her childhood filled her with nostalgia. She was sad about leaving Mussoorie forever. It was a place where she had spent nine golden years of her life and where she had also met Robin, the first crush of her life. It was a difficult thought to part with. The car which brought her from Mussoorie suddenly ground to halt with a jerk and brought Lalsa out of her reverie.

2

Home Sweet Home

Lalsa had reached home. When she entered her house, she noticed that it had been beautifully decorated with balloons and lights. Sanjay Uncle received her with a bouquet and said, "Welcome back, Lalsa *beta*!"

Lalsa took the bouquet and hugged Sanjay uncle lovingly. Sanjay uncle was her father's elder brother and the most revered man in the family. He was the man through whom Lalsa and her mother would get anything done from his father, as Lalsa's father never dared to say no to Sanjay.

Behind him stood, her entire family–all her cousins, friends, uncles and aunts were there. The extended family stood along with her beaming parents. She was overwhelmed by this grand gesture. They all chatted till late in the night, revisited old memories and indulged in the delicious food cooked by Lalsa's mother. Lalsa realised that sweet memories are like a precious treasure box which everyone loves to open from time to time. Every family gathering is also a chance to revisit the same incidents and same jokes with the same enthusiasm and enjoyment and strangely they never become jaded. The pleasure derived by revisiting such moments spent with dear ones never lessens. Lalsa noticed that Sanjay Uncle was not at all participating in the conversation. He seemed withdrawn and sad.

"Sanjay Uncle, are you all right? Why are you looking weak?" Lalsa was genuinely concerned.

"I am fine *beta*!" Sanjay answered with a fake smile but Lalsa was not convinced. She decided to talk to her mother about him afterwards.

Next day, Lalsa's father went out of station on a routine business trip for three days. Her mother told Lalsa to get ready, as she had planned to take her out to Roshnara Club for a swim and lunch in. She reluctantly got ready on her mother's insistence and accompanied her to the club. Her reluctance was mainly due to her being preoccupied with Robin's indifference towards her. He had not bothered to call her up ever since they had parted in Mussoorie.

When Lalsa entered the pool, four girls were already swimming. After the swim, she felt better. While having lunch, she saw a girl sitting with a lady and staring at her with a smile. She was very tall, with beautiful features and very long hair. Lalsa recalled that she was one of the girls swimming with her in the pool. She did not want to appear rude, so she returned the smile. Lalsa's mother told her that she knew both the mother and the daughter as they were frequent visitors to the club.

After they finished lunch, the girl came to meet them along with her mother at their table.

"Hi, Aunty! How are you?" she asked Lalsa's mother, Kanta but her eyes were fixed on Lalsa.

"I am good, Shikha. Hello Vrinda, come let me introduce you to my daughter, Lalsa," Kanta said with a smile.

Shikha and Lalsa shook hands with each other. Their mothers got busy with their own conversation and soon both the girls also started chatting. Lalsa found Shikha to be a vivacious, warm and a friendly girl. In fact, Lalsa felt quite comfortable with her. Lalsa invited Shikha home for lunch and Shikha was more than happy to accept the invitation.

Next day, both of them had lunch together and chatted till late in the evening. They instantly grew fond of each other. Shikha told her that she lived in a joint family along with her parents, her uncle and his son under one roof; her cousin was older than her and no less than a real brother to her.

Soon, Lalsa shared everything about herself with Shikha, but didn't confide about Robin. Gradually, they started meeting every day. Shikha would suggest one or another interesting programme which the two new friends would look forward to eagerly. They were together virtually every day.

Meanwhile, three weeks had passed and there was still no word from Robin in the three weeks that had passed. She had called Robin several times but each time the phone was disconnected. The sorrow of being ignored was lessened because of Shikha's entertaining company that had all her attention. Shikha was enamoured by Lalsa. She would keep looking at her without blinking her eyes. Many a time she would hold her hand and kiss it lovingly. Shikha was completely obsessed by her. She kept Lalsa's picture in her wallet and Lalsa on the other hand was amazed to see Shikha's fondness for her. Shikha would always dissuade her from going anywhere without her. At times, she would jokingly suggest that both of them get married as they were spending so much good time together.

She once told her, "Lalsa, I will not let you go anywhere. You will have to marry one of my cousins." She talked appreciatively of her cousin Drishtant very often and seemed to hold him in great awe. She also suggested that Lalsa meet Drishtant but Lalsa turned down the suggestion as she was not interested.

3

A New Thrill

Shikha invited Lalsa home for her birthday party. Lalsa had not visited her place. Her driver dropped her off at Shikha's house. Lalsa looked stunning in a black top which reached above her knees that she had paired with black leggings.

Shikha lived in Punjabi Bagh in a massive house with a sprawling garden. Lalsa lived in Rajinder Nagar, not very far from Shikha's place.

The party was held in a palatial drawing room decorated in luxurious western style with four seating arrangements and exquisite decor. The exclusive collection of paintings, the branded show pieces with an opulent Persian carpet laid in the centre of the floor all added to the elegance of the drawing room.

Shikha had invited only her friends and cousins; therefore, the crowd was fairly young at the party though her parents, uncle and her cousin, Drishtant, who lived in the same house, were also present for the cake-cutting ceremony. Following that, Shikha's parents and her uncle left the party.

Shikha introduced Lalsa to her other friends and cousins. Her cousin, Drishtant, looked strikingly handsome in a steel grey blazer with a light grey shirt and black jeans. He was around six feet tall with strong facial features and long hair till his shoulders tied into a ponytail. Shikha told her that after he completed his graduation, he had joined the family business of cable manufacturing.

"Hi!" he said and looked intensely into Lalsa's eyes while shaking hands with her. Lalsa was impressed by his confidence made obvious with his hand shake and courtesy. Although, she could see the lust for her in every boy's eyes, he was the only one to shake hands with her with such charm. In the corner of the room, a temporary wooden dancing floor had been put together. The music started playing and everybody started dancing except Drishtant who stood sipping beer in one corner of the bar. Lalsa could see that he had fixed his gaze on her and even Lalsa could not stop herself from looking at him.

At 8:00 p.m., Kanta called Lalsa and asked her to return as her father was back home after three days and wanted to meet her. Shikha didn't want her to leave but Lalsa insisted and left the party. When Lalsa reached home, her father was waiting for her at the dinner table. He had brought lots of chocolates and a perfume for her. Lalsa didn't feel like eating anything but gave company to her parents by sitting and chatting with them.

Lalsa thought about Drishtant while trying to sleep. She was yet to meet a more handsome boy. He seemed to be strong and composed. She was sure that he was also smitten by her good looks. She recalled that Robin was also very good looking but Drishtant was stunningly handsome. Although, the thought of Robin made her feel guilty, she decided to switch off her thoughts and sleep.

Next morning, she got up late and while she was eating her breakfast, Shikha called her. She told her that she was planning to go for a swim and would pick her up on her way to the club. Lalsa agreed as she didn't have anything else to do.

An hour later, Shikha was outside her house, waiting for her in the car. Lalsa got into the car and to her surprise, found Drishant behind the wheel.

"Hi Lalsa, actually I had to clear my monthly bills at the club so I thought that you guys can also accompany me." Lalsa smiled as in her heart she knew that he had come to see her. She felt happy to see his restlessness which implied that he had started liking her. Why else would he have attempted to meet her again!

In the club, he cleared his bills and then joined them to chat and have lunch together. He was very curious to know everything about Lalsa. She also enjoyed his company as he was very witty and caring. He had big dreams for himself and wanted to go abroad for his Master's. After returning from abroad he wanted to start his own business. She could see the passion in his eyes to do something big. He appeared to be a very strong person with clarity about his goals, and there was no doubt that Lalsa liked him too.

Before going off to sleep that night, she remembered Robin and wished he were a strong person like Drishtant. She felt being cheated and dejected because of his indifference. Robin had to leave for London from Mussoorie abruptly because of his father's sudden death. However, Lalsa wished that he stayed in touch with her at least over the phone. She sighed and consoled herself by reassuring herself that maybe everything that happened, happened for the better. Maybe Robin had been a wrong choice for her.

The next day, Shikha planned a day out to watch a movie. As expected, Drishtant also accompanied them. Lalsa noticed that he was very possessive about both the girls. He made it a point to protect them from a passing man's touch and gaze. Lalsa glowed in this sense of possessiveness and care. No one had been so possessive about her as she didn't have a brother, and her father was too busy to be possessive the way Drishtant was.

Gradually, meeting Drishtant and Shikha together became a regular affair. There was not even a single day when Drishtant would not come to see her. Even if he was busy during the day, he would come at night with Shikha, and all three of them would go for a drive. Lalsa also started looking forward to meeting him every day.

Her mother noticed the increasing proximity of Lalsa and Drishtant but she didn't object. Shikha would deliberately praise Drishtant in front of Lalsa's mother saying that he was the brightest boy of the family. Her mother had always dreamt of a good looking son-in-law as she was very proud of Lalsa's looks. She grew fond of Drishtant not only because of his looks but also because of his courteous behaviour. He seemed to be a well groomed and respectful guy from an affluent family. She couldn't have expected more than that in her future son-in-law.

One day, Shikha came along with Drishtant to pick Lalsa up in the evening. They went for a drive. After a while Shikha told Drishtant to drop her at another friend's house and pick her back after half an hour. Lalsa felt thrilled. Her heart fluttered with excitement on being alone with Drishtant.

Drishtant turned back, looked deep into her eyes and said smilingly, "Can you please come to the front seat?"

"Sure," said Lalsa in a low voice and got into the front seat.

Drishtant played the song–"*All Of Me Loves All Of You*..." Lalsa blushed as she knew that something exciting was in the offing.

Drishtant stopped the car on the side of the road. He held Lalsa's hand in his and said, "Lalsa, I love you! You will be the first and last love of my life. You are always in my thoughts, in my dreams and now I want you to always be in my life. Please tell me you also love me, please Lalsa!" Drishtant pleaded.

Lalsa didn't know what to say. Everything was unfolding so quickly that she was at a loss for words.

"Say something, Lalsa! You are scaring me by not saying anything!" Drishtant sounded worried.

Lalsa started giggling and said, "Please give me some time before committing anything." Lalsa was amused to see him so helpless.

"I hope there is nobody else in your life?" Drishtant asked worriedly.

Lalsa was enjoying his impatience.

"No!" she said with a smile.

"Thank God!"

Lalsa had a hearty laugh. "Now let's pick up Shikha from her friend's house, otherwise we will get late."

"Okay. But don't take too long to give me your reply," Drishtant requested as they drove off.

4

Why Didn't You Smile?

Drishtant and Shikha dropped Lalsa back home. Her mother, who was waiting for her, sat alone flipping through the pages of her wedding album. Lalsa went and sat near her to gaze at and flip through her parents' wedding photos.

"Mom, you had a love marriage, right? Then why do you look so serious in all your wedding photographs? Why didn't you smile?" Lalsa quipped.

Kanta heaved a deep sigh, then smiled and said, "It is a strange story."

"Oh! Must be an interesting one! Please tell me, Mom!" Lalsa insisted.

Without any hesitation, Kanta started narrating the story and Lalsa was all ears.

Lalsa's mother, Kanta belonged to a humble family and had four younger siblings–two sisters and two brothers. Her father worked in a private company and his income failed to meet the needs of his family. After completing her graduation Kanta also started working in a private company as a typist to supplement the family income. She was twenty when she met Vijay. He was very good looking and would come to her bus stop every day on his motorbike to see Kanta. He was a jobless graduate who had lost his mother, and his father was bed ridden. His elder brother Sanjay, an accountant in a big private company met all their expenses.

Kanta liked Vijay and secretly enjoyed his attention. Soon Vijay started picking her up and dropping her off. They didn't have money to spend on each other as Vijay was jobless and Kanta had to give her entire salary to her father to cater to the needs of the family. In order to spend time with each other, they would often sit in a park for a while and chat or walk together. Sometimes Kanta would cook something special for him, which they would eat together in the park. There were times when Kanta would skip the office for a few hours and go to the movies with Vijay.

One day, Vijay took Kanta to his house and introduced her to his brother and father. Both of them liked Kanta instantly. Sanjay, Vijay's elder brother grew fond of her and treated her like a younger sister. Five years of this interaction whizzed by. Sanjay remained unmarried and Vijay was still struggling to set up a new business of pest control for government and private companies. By then, Kanta was a regular visitor at Vijay's house. As a gesture of kindness, she ensured that there was enough food in their fridge. Whenever possible, she would cook extra food for all of them and store that in their fridge. The gesture was highly appreciated by the family. Talking to the doctor and monitoring Vijay's father's treatment became a duty she tacitly took on.

A year later, Sanjay got married and Vijay's business began to grow, fuelled by big orders from both government and private companies. Once Vijay's business started flourishing, Vijay and Kanta decided to get married. Their relationship had the approval of Kanta's family too.

With just two days left for the wedding, Kanta's relatives arrived to celebrate another chapter of her life. Amidst all the rituals, a strange incident occurred. Kanta was standing in the verandah of her house when she saw three men standing at the door and asking for her.

"I am Kanta. Are you the tent *wala*?" Kanta asked them.

"No we are Maninder's brothers," a man who looked like a body builder answered in a loud voice.

"Then what should I do? I don't know any Maninder," Kanta replied.

"Ask Vijay who is Maninder. He knows her very well."

"Then go to Vijay. Why are you talking to me?"

"We are talking to you because you are marrying him."

"How does that concern you?"

"Vijay befriended our sister, Maninder six months back and started roaming around everywhere with her on his motorbike. A month back he married her secretly and now he is marrying you."

Kanta could not believe what she heard and felt dizzy and weak in her knees. Her mind went blank as she struggled to find her voice. "What proof do you have that he has married your sister?"

"See this paper," one of them said and took out a paper from his pocket.

Kanta examined the paper carefully. The handwriting was quiet similar to Vijay's. It was a written confession by Vijay that he had secretly married Maninder in a temple and that she was his wife.

"Even if Vijay has written it, why should I believe that it is true? Do you have any legal evidence?"

None of the men answered.

"Just leave my house or I will call the police." Kanta threatened angrily. Meanwhile, her relatives came out to see what had transpired and why Kanta was shouting. Looking at her relatives, the three men talked among themselves and said, "We are leaving but remember you will regret this marriage all your life. He has cheated our sister and now he is cheating on you."

Saying this, they left the house.

"Who were they? What were they saying?" one of the uncles asked Kanta in a concerned voice.

"Nothing, Uncle. They were warning me about one shopkeeper who had cheated them," Kanta lied. She didn't want to create a scene. But in her heart, Kanta was highly disturbed. She called Vijay a couple of times but he didn't pick up the phone. As her anxiety mounted, she called up his brother Sanjay who answered the phone immediately.

"Hello, Kanta! Has Vijay picked up a fight with you?"

"Why are you asking me this Sanjay *bhaiya*?" Kanta asked worriedly.

"Because he has locked himself in his room and is not opening the door. Tell me what has happened?"

"*Bhaiya*, I want to meet you right now," said Kanta.

"Why? What has happened? Is everything alright?"

"I don't know. That's why I want to meet you," Kanta answered hurriedly.

"Okay! Why don't you come over right now. Nobody is at home," said Sanjay.

"Okay, I am coming."

Kanta reached Vijay's house and apprised Sanjay about the whole episode and also showed him the piece of paper with Vijay's confession.

"I just can't believe this." Sanjay was shattered after reading the note.

"Let's ask Vijay directly. He will have to tell us the truth." Sanjay rushed towards Vijay's room aggressively.

"Vijay open the door. Kanta has come to see you." Sanjay said while thumping the door.

After a while, Vijay opened the door. He looked very upset and his eyes were red as if he had been crying.

Kanta became more worried, seeing him in this condition. She was sure by then that there was something seriously amiss and expected some bad news.

"Vijay see this note. Have you written it?" asked Sanjay while showing him the paper.

"Yes, I have written it," said Vijay with tearful eyes.

"What do you mean? Did you...did you...have you married someone else when you are supposed to marry Kanta?" Sanjay spluttered with shock and Kanta was speechless. She was too scared to ask anything.

"No, I didn't marry that girl," said Vijay.

"Then why did you write this note? Do you know any Maninder? Tell us the truth," said Sanjay in an assertive voice.

"I met Maninder six months back at my friend Sunil's house. She is a friend of his sister. She had come from Punjab to find a job in Delhi. Sunil requested me to help her in finding a job. I talked to a few people and accompanied her to one or two places for interviews as she was new to Delhi. I don't know when she stared liking me. When she came to know about my marriage with Kanta, she insisted that I call off the wedding and marry her. But I refused to do that. This morning, when I was sitting in my office, three men entered my room. One of them took out a pistol and said that they were Maninder's brothers. They forced me to write this note and threatened me that if I married someone else, they would kill me. My only fault is that I tried to help that girl."

"I knew it. I was sure that you would never betray Kanta," Sanjay said heaving a sigh of relief but Kanta was exasperated, still unable to absorb the revelation.

"But why didn't you tell me anything about that girl? You were meeting her and also accompanying her to various places but you never spoke a word about it. Why were you so secretive? Aren't your intentions equally questionable? It seems you met this girl everyday but kept me in the dark. Why? Why should I believe anything you say now?" Kanta asked furiously.

"I admit my fault. Please forgive me. I didn't tell you about this girl, fearing that you may misunderstand me. But in future, I will never commit such a mistake. I will never meet this girl again and never hide anything from you," Vijay said nervously.

"Yes Kanta, please forgive him. I can assure you that he will never cheat on you. Forget about this episode. You have known him for six years now. How can he betray you? I myself shall go to the police station and lodge a complaint about this girl and her brothers and ask for police protection till your wedding," said Sanjay, placing his hand on her shoulder reassuringly.

Kanta forgave Vijay but in her heart she was still tense which is why she looked so serious in the wedding photos. The tension lasted through the wedding evening and lingered on. "But," with a sigh of relief Kanta said, "since our wedding, I have not heard your Dad mention anything about Maninder."

"Did those people create any problems thereafter?" Lalsa asked curiously.

"No, not so far!"

"Thank God!"

"Mom, tell me what is wrong with Sanjay Uncle? Is he unwell? That day he looked very different," Lalsa asked worryingly.

"Yes, you are right Lalsa! I don't know why but he has alienated himself from everyone. Earlier, he was a very social person and used to visit our house very frequently but nowadays, he seldom goes anywhere.

"I think you should ask Dad to talk to him."

"Yes, I will!"

"Okay, Mom. I am feeling very hungry now so please give me something to eat." Lalsa stood up impatiently as she wanted to be alone to indulge in the sweet memory of all that Drishtant had declared about his emotions.

5

Love Blossoms

The night was special. A gradual realisation dawned upon Lalsa that she had begun to have feelings for Drishtant. It was very difficult to turn down a person who in Lalsa's eyes was just perfect. He had completely occupied Lalsa's mind and made her forget about Robin–the first crush of her life. She was very disappointed with Robin who had ended his relationship with her abruptly. Otherwise also in her heart, she knew that they didn't have a future together. Her conservative Punjabi parents would have never agreed to let her continue relationship with Robin, an Anglo-Indian boy.

But in the case of Drishtant, she was aware that her mother knew their family well and also liked him. Therefore, her parents would happily approve of her relationship with Drishtant. Her heart began to melt for him and she convinced herself that it was hard for any girl to remain unaffected by Drishtant's charismatic personality. Therefore, she also fell for him.

Next morning, Lalsa woke up feeling unwell. To make things worse Lalsa's mobile fell down in the toilet and stopped working.

After expressing his love for Lalsa, Drishtant was desperate to talk to her and know her reaction. He decided to seek Shikha's help. Shikha visited Lalsa's house and delivered a box to her.

"What is this?" Lalsa was inquisitive.

"I don't know! Drishtant asked me to give it to you."

Lalsa ripped open the packaging to find a fully charged mobile phone with a new SIM card in the box.

Suddenly, the mobile started ringing. It was Drishtant on the line.

"Hi, Drishtant you need not give me such an expensive gift. Also, I hope to resume using my old mobile soon."

"Don't be formal with me, Lalsa! I couldn't wait any more to talk to you. I want to come to see you right now. Can I?"

Lalsa told him not to come as she didn't want her mother to get suspicious unnecessarily. At night, Lalsa admitted her love for Drishtant and they talked at a length on the phone. Both of them had so much to share that night stretched into the day, and they finally hung up at 4 a.m.

She got up late in the morning. She was still in her bed when she got a phone call from Drishtant.

"Hi, Lalsa. How are you now?" He was concerned.

"Better," a smile flashed across her face.

"I am missing you. Can't you come out?" Drishtant sounded desperate.

"No! Not at all. My parents will kill me."

"Okay then, just come out in your balcony."

"Why? Where are you?" Lalsa asked excitedly while throwing aside her blanket. She hurriedly wore her slippers and rushed towards her balcony with a fluttering heart and her mobile stuck to her ear.

To her amazement, Drishtant had parked his car, right in front of her house from where he could see her clearly.

He waved at her with a smile. Lalsa was very happy with his surprise visit.

"Now, don't keep standing with an open mouth. Sit down on the swing near you, otherwise you will get tired," said Drishtant.

Lalsa laughed heartily and sat on her favourite swing. She was very fond of swings. Her mother had especially ordered that swing for her. They kept talking for half an hour across the balcony. Fortunately, nobody disturbed Lalsa during their conversation. Instead of feeling satiated, both of them had become very restless to meet each other.

"Can't I come inside?"

"No, my mom and the house help both are inside the house," Lalsa said laughingly. She was enjoying his restlessness.

While they were talking, suddenly they saw her mother going out somewhere along with her house help. The house help was carrying flowers, fruits and milk in his hands.

Thankfully she didn't notice his car as she was going towards the opposite direction.

"Oh, today is Monday! My mother is going to the temple," Lalsa said.

"Your house help is also accompanying her," Drishtant said happily.

"Yes, because she can't carry all the stuff she has to offer to Lord Shiva in the temple."

"Okay, how long is she going to take?"

"The temple is nearby, so not more than 20 to 30 minutes," Lalsa guessed.

"Oh, wow! We have ample time. I am coming inside," Drishtant said enthusiastically.

"No, no!" Lalsa was excited but a bit scared also.

"Yes! Yes! Come down and open the door," Drishtant said persuasively.

Lalsa rushed down to open the door. Drishtant locked the door, hugged her tight to his chest and started kissing her frantically without waiting to sit somewhere.

"Hey! Let me be! Keep away from me, you will also catch the viral."

"I am already suffering from the *lovaria* virus. You know, only you can cure me."

Drishtant curved down his lips like a sad baby. Both of them guffawed.

After ten minutes, Lalsa had to literally push him out of her house fearing her mother would be back any time now. She knew that she would not have any explanation to justify his visit.

It was a thrilling experience. Both of them were very happy. Drishtant promised her that if possible, he would come to see her the next day also.

Next day, her mother had a kitty party but she was reluctant to go because of Lalsa's sickness. Lalsa persuaded her to go as she didn't have fever anymore. Lalsa informed Drishtant that he could come to see her between 1:00 p.m. and 3:00 p.m. but the only hurdle was her house help, who would still be in the house.

Drishtant parked his car outside Lalsa's house at 1:30 p.m., and waited for Lalsa's call to go inside the house.

Lalsa went down to look for her house help who was working in the kitchen.

"Ram *Bhaiya*, tell me do we have apples at home?"

"Yes, *Didi*. Should I cut some for you?"

"No, no," said Lalsa with disappointment.

"Okay, tell me do we have pomegranate?"

"No, *Didi*."

"Good, take this money and get pomegranate for me."

"Okay, *Didi*," said Ram and left for the market. She immediately called up Drishtant, asking him to come inside. Lalsa was feeling happy to see that Drishtant was as eager as she was to meet her.

"How much time will he take to come back?"

"About half an hour as the market is a bit far away. What are you carrying in your hand?" Lalsa asked, noticing the packet in his hand.

"This is your favourite butter chicken and mint naan."

"You know in the hostel, most of the times, we were served bland chicken that too with bread or rice. This is the reason why I love to eat naan and butter chicken. But now I am sick, so I should not eat such heavy food."

"Don't worry. I am going to feed you with my own hands, so it will not harm you." Drishtant said lovingly while unpacking the food.

"Okay. I know you are not going to listen to me," Lalsa surrendered.

They sat in the lobby and Drishtant fed her with his own hands. Lalsa gobbled some food and after 15 minutes she asked him to leave.

"Please take away the remaining food, otherwise my house help will get suspicious." Lalsa warned Drishtant.

"Okay, I will leave but first get up and give me a tight hug."

Lalsa stood up. Drishtant hugged her tight and planted a warm kiss on her forehead and said, "Get well soon, honey!"

The minute he decided to go out, the door bell rang up. Lalsa's face turned pale. She had no option but to open the door as there was no one else in the house.

To her horror, it was her mother. She saw Drishtant with food packets in his hands.

"Hi, Aunty! Actually I was passing by and Shikha asked me to drop these packets here. Okay, now I would like to leave." He hurriedly kept the food packets on the table. Without waiting for her answer, he hurried towards the door.

Kanta didn't say anything and went to her room. Lalsa also went upstairs to her room but in her heart she knew that her mother was too smart and must have understood the reality. She decided that instead of giving any explanation, she should wait for her mother's interrogation.

Kanta came to her room after half an hour.

"How is your fever now?" she asked while touching her forehead.

"I think I am fine now."

"Hmm...I know why you are fine now," she said with a smile.

Lalsa knew what she meant although she was relieved to see that her mother smiling instead of scolding her.

Kanta sat on her bed near her and said, "I know everything. He comes here every day. Don't I understand his intentions?" She said with a smile and continued, "I like him and his family is also known to us. I don't have any objection regarding your relationship with Drishtant. They are nice people but you are very young. At least complete your education.

Then she raised Lalsa's chin with one hand looked and said, "One more thing–always be careful and never cross your limits. I hope you understand."

Lalsa got up on her knees on the bed and hugged her. "Yes, Mom, I understand. Don't worry, I am your daughter, and I will never let you down."

"Okay, I think you must have had lunch with him, so now take rest. I am going down to have my lunch."

"But why did you come back so early without having food?"

"You are sick. That's why I didn't want to leave you alone for long," Kanta answered.

"Oh! So sweet of you, love you Mom," Lalsa hugged her mother again.

Lalsa was dying to share the news of her mother's approval of their relationship with Drishtant. When she told him this, he was overwhelmed by the news. He decided not to share it with anyone except Shikha and Shikha's mother, Vrinda who was not only a mother-figure but also a friend to him. Shikha was over-excited after hearing the news and so was her mother. Vrinda advised them to not share anything with anyone, as their relationship was very raw. Therefore, it would be best if they waited for sometime to be sure of their decision. Drishtant started visiting Lalsa's house more often to take Lalsa out in the presence of her mother. Both of them were having the best time of their lives.

6

Take My Permission First

Lalsa secured a good score in her school exams. She had always wanted to be a fashion designer and launch her own line of couture. Her parents were happy with her decision because they always wanted her to be financially independent. It was her dream to get admission in London College of Fashion Designing. Her father had promised to send her to London for a Fashion Designing course but Drishtant wouldn't let her to go so far from her. Finally, she got admission in Pearl Academy which was not very far from her house. On the first day of college, Drishtant gifted Lalsa a beautiful diamond studded watch with a note that said:

My love,

This gift is to assure you that with every tick of this watch, someone's heart is beating only for you. It will remind you that time is ticking away fast and someone is desperately waiting for you with a wish to be together till eternity.

Your heart is my humble abode.

With love,

Drishtant

Lalsa felt flattered by his expression of immense love. Drishtant was madly in love with her. He would always surprise her with beautiful gifts and interesting programmes. After office, all his time was for Lalsa. He would accompany her everywhere, even for buying her clothes. His obsession with Lalsa was increasing with each passing day.

Many a time, he would come to her college unexpectedly just to check on her. At first, Lalsa liked his attention and possessiveness but gradually she started feeling embarrassed and irritated. He started placing restrictions on her clothes also. He insisted she wear long tops with jeans instead of skirts and short tops. Lalsa was not used to such restrictions as her parents had never stopped her from doing anything but now, because of Drishtant, she was trying to mould herself according to his whims and fancies.

Festive time arrived and Dussehra holidays started. One day, Lalsa's mother invited all her cousins for dinner. After dinner, all of them decided to go to a disco.

Lalsa had never been to a disco, so she was looking forward to having a good time at the disco. Everybody decided to share the expenses. Lalsa went upstairs to get ready and talk to Drishtant before leaving, as she knew that she would get late and Drishtant would keep waiting for her.

"Hi, Drishtant."

"Hi! You took so long to call. Why?"

"My cousins are still here and we are going to a disco." Lalsa sounded very excited.

"What did you say? Where are you going?" Drishtant rasped with anger.

"To a disco. Why, what happened?" Lalsa was surprised as she never expected such a reaction from Drishtant.

"Are you mad? With whose permission are you going there?" he said loudly.

"I asked my mom and she is okay with it."

"Oh my god! What a strange family! Your mother may not have a problem because she would have never ever been to any disco. Desperate boys and girls go there to get sozzled and flirt with each other, so you are certainly not going."

"What do you mean? Everybody is waiting for me downstairs. I am the one to make the plan. How can I duck out now?"

"I don't know! I can't let you go there. You will have to say no." Drishtant was adamant.

"I can't, please Drishtant try to understand."

"Okay, then go to hell." Drishtant hung up on her.

Lalsa called him again.

"Please Drishtant, please let me go this time. I won't go again."

"No, not at any cost," Drishtant was firm.

"Please, Drishtant!" Lalsa felt very helpless

"If you are so desperate, then go but don't dare call me again." Drishtant was exasperated. He hung up again.

Lalsa started crying. She was feeling miserable. She wanted to go but didn't have the courage to annoy Drishtant. She washed her face and went downstairs.

"Hey guys, I can't go. Suddenly, my stomach has started aching. I don't think I would be able to accompany you, so you please carry on!"

All of them including her mother were amazed at her behaviour.

"What happened, dear? Take medicine and go!" Kanta advised.

"No, Mom. The pain is aggravating. I don't want to spoil the programme for everyone."

She persuaded everyone to leave. After all of them had left, she went upstairs as it was difficult for her to hide her tears anymore. Her mother didn't say anything but in her heart, she knew that Lalsa was lying.

Lalsa called up Drishtant again but he didn't pick up the phone so she sent him a message: *"I didn't go anywhere. I am just lying in my bed and sulking. Hope you are happy now."*

Drishtant called her up immediately. But Lalsa was too upset to talk.

"I shall call you in the morning. Good night." She said sadly and disconnected the phone.

She kept tossing and turning on the bed as she cried till 4 in the morning. She had always been a very independent girl who had always taken her own decisions. Her parents had always been very supportive and she'd always had it her way. This was the first time that someone else had taken full charge of her and started making decisions on her behalf. She felt stifled but her love for Drishtant was greater than her own sense of independence, that's why she submitted to his authoritative behaviour. Every morning, Lalsa felt almost duty bound to call up Drishtant immediately after she woke up. However, that morning she got up late and didn't feel like talking to him, so she decided to call him a bit later. Drishtant didn't call her either. Around 11:30 a.m., she got a message from him: *"Sleeping beauty, if you are awake by now then please come out of the house. I am waiting impatiently in my car outside your house. Please come fast."*

Lalsa was alone at home as her father was out of station and her mother had just left for the market. She didn't feel like meeting him as she was still very upset but didn't have the guts to annoy him by saying no. Her love for Drishtant overpowered her self-respect and anger. She wondered how much authority had she already given to Drishtant to rule over her.

Drishtant was sitting in his car. As soon as he saw her coming, he smiled and greeted her normally, as if nothing had happened the night before. She sat down in the car next to him.

"Just look down, near your feet." Drishtant said smilingly.

Lalsa looked down and saw a carry bag lying near her feet.

"See, there is a surprise for you."

Lalsa looked at him, confused. She was unable to understand his intentions.

"Don't worry, dear. It is not a bomb. Just open it and see for yourself."

Lalsa opened the bag unwillingly. There were two perfume bottles and a delicate bracelet. Lalsa looked at his face again to figure out what was going on in his mind.

"Why are you looking at me? It is for you. Just wear the bracelet and show me, how it looks on your beautiful wrist," Drishtant said excitedly.

Lalsa didn't know how to react. She was disappointed and sad because of the previous night, yet was touched by his affection. Her heart began to melt and her eyes grew moist. Drishtant hugged her and planted a kiss on her cheek.

"Sorry, dear, but I am like that. I can't let anyone else touch you. Hope you understand me and my love! Do you?"

Lalsa nodded in affirmation.

"Thank you," said Drishtant in a low voice and kissed her forehead. By then, Lalsa had completely forgiven him.

7

Trouble in Paradise

Lalsa was very excited as her cousin, Saumya, who lived in Lucknow was getting married in Delhi. The groom and his parents were from New York. A week-long celebration had begun and Lalsa caught everyone's attention because of her dancing skills. One could tell all the boys wanted to befriend her. Her mother even got a marriage proposal for her from a very rich diamond merchant's son from Mumbai. But she turned down the proposal saying that Lalsa was too young to get married.

Lalsa was asked to invite all her friends to the cocktail. Shikha and Drishtant attended all the functions. Throughout all the functions, Drishtant was upset. He didn't like boys hovering around Lalsa. He didn't want her to dance in front of other people and wear short dresses at the functions.

It was a cocktail where all young girls were supposed to wear western dresses. Lalsa looked very attractive in a black and gold long dress with a side slit till her thigh. Whenever she put her foot forward, her well-shaped right leg peeped out. Everyone was dancing and enjoying while Drishtant was not on the dance floor. He was at the bar, making his drink, when he heard two boys talking rotten stuff about all the girls.

One of them said, "Have you seen that beautiful girl in the black dress? Look at her legs, so sexy."

Realising that the boys were talking about Lalsa, Drishtant got furious.

"You scoundrels! Better mind your tongue or you will never be able to use your tongue again," Drishtant rasped angrily.

The boys got scared and immediately scurried away.

He went on the floor and mumbled in Lalsa's ears, "Come out, I want to talk to you. I am waiting in my car."

Lalsa didn't know what to do. It would have been very awkward to leave the party and go out in the presence of her parents. She came down from the dancing floor and went to the toilet from where she called up Drishtant.

"What happened, Drishtant? Are you okay?"

"First of all, you get out of there and come downstairs then I will let you know." Drishtant said with a sting in his voice.

"Are you out of your mind? My father is also here. How can I skip the function and come out?"

"I don't know but you will have to come out otherwise I am leaving."

"Please Drishtant, don't do this to me. Why are you so angry? What has happened? Tell me please."

"I hate you! I am leaving and don't show me your face again." Drishtant yelled and disconnected the phone. After that, Lalsa kept calling him but his phone was switched off.

Lalsa was very upset. She didn't eat anything and wanted to go back home as soon as possible.

Immediately after reaching her bedroom, she called Drishtant. His phone was on but he wasn't taking her calls.

She wrote a message to Drishtant: "*Why aren't you taking my call?*"

"*Stop bothering me. I don't want to continue my relationship with you.*"

"*But why?*"

"*I hate girls who wear skimpy clothes.*"

"*What do you mean? Are you mad? How dare you talk like this to me?*"

"*Don't pretend to be so innocent. You know what I am talking about. All the boys were passing remarks on your legs.*"

"*I don't believe that. It is your own weird imagination. Nobody said anything to me about my dress.*"

"*You mean to say that I am lying? Just get lost.*"

That was Drishtant's last message after which he switched off the phone.

Lalsa kept crying the whole night. In the morning, her face, especially her eyes told the story of her heart. Her mother sensed that she was upset because of Drishtant as she had seen him go on the dancing floor and talk to Lalsa after which Lalsa was upset during the entire function.

"What happened, Lalsa? Why are you crying?" asked her mother while moving her fingers through her hair.

"Nothing much, Mom. I have a bad headache," said Lalsa.

"Are you trying to fool your mother, Lalsa? Why don't you stop talking to him? There is no point continuing a relationship with a person who cannot keep you happy. I will tell him not to come to our house again," her mother said angrily.

"No, Mom. Don't do that. We will sort out everything together, you need not worry."

"Okay, but you know that neither I nor your father can see tears in your eyes. In future, if he hurts you again, I will not let you talk to him."

"Okay, Mom," Lalsa hugged her mother tight, "Thanks for your love and support." She was touched by her mother's concern for her.

Next day, it was Saumya's wedding. She was getting married to a renowned painter–Parichay. He was soft spoken, and a thorough gentleman. Lalsa was very upset but tried her best to hide her grief throughout the wedding. Shikha attended the wedding but Drishtant kept away and didn't even call Lalsa.

The couple was scheduled to go to Europe for fifteen days on their honeymoon after a week. But surprisingly, the day after their wedding, they went to an exotic resort in Haryana for two days.

After two days, Saumya came back and visited Lalsa's house for *pug phera*–a ceremony where a married girl visits her maternal home for the first time after getting married. Saumya's own house was in Lucknow, therefore, she visited Lalsa's house and all the cousins were invited for lunch. Everyone insisted Saumya reveal where had they suddenly disappeared in Haryana. They wanted to know the tiniest detail of her two-day stay in Haryana. Saumya narrated her experience and everyone listened to her as the night slipped into dawn.

8

The Patch-Up

Lalsa got engrossed for some time in her cousin's narration but was extremely sad deep down because of Drishtant's behaviour. She missed him but was too hurt to talk to him.

Drishtant didn't talk to her for an entire week. Ultimately, Shikha told her mother Vrinda to intervene as Drishtant was not ready to budge. Drishtant was very close to Vrinda. After the death of his mother, Vrinda was the mother-figure for him. She did everything for him that a parent would do– from preparing snacks for his tiffin, helping him in his homework to attending parents-teachers meeting. Drishant had a very profound emotional connect with Vrinda. He called her Vindy. She was very happy to know about his relationship with Lalsa as she herself was very fond of her. When Shikha informed Vrinda about the fight between Drishtant and Lalsa, she decided to discuss it with him.

It was late in the evening when Vrinda entered his room. Drishtant had just come back from the office. He was lying on the bed and his face looked forlorn.

"Drishtant, should I bring something for you to eat?" Vrinda asked affectionately. She sat down on his bed and started massaging his head gently with her fingers.

"No, Vindy Mom," answered Drishtant without opening his eyes.

"Why are you so upset, son? Is it something to do with Lalsa?"

"I know, Shikha must have told you everything."

"Yes, I know about the incident but how is she at fault? She was not responsible for the behaviour of those boys. Why are you angry with her?"

"Why did she wear those provoking clothes? Doesn't she know how boys are these days. In spite of my repeated warnings, she chose to wear skimpy clothes. I can't bear this nonsense," Drishtant said.

"Nowadays, it is absolutely normal for all girls to wear clothes of their choice. She is not doing something exceptional, Drishtant. She has the liberty to dress up as she pleases, like other girls. You are unnecessarily blowing this out of proportion because of your own insecurity."

"Yes, I know all girls wear such clothes but when someone misbehaves with them, then the whole society cries foul and blame men," Drishtant said bitterly.

"Drishtant, you are being completely insensitive. Men misbehave with girls because of their sick mind. That has very little to do with the way girls dress."

"But if she has to live with me, then she will have to act according to my likes and dislikes," Drishtant sounded stubborn.

"Are you talking about a slave or a girl whom you wish to marry?" Vrinda fumed and continued, "Sorry Drishtant, if you have such a mentality, then no girl would like to be your wife. Every girl expects love and respect from her partner. If you continue to behave in this manner, then you will lose her forever. Don't try to possess her like a pet that should always follow your commands. Just let your love bloom in the air of freedom. Strengthen your relation with her through liberation and not control. You have hurt her. Before it gets too late, call her up," Vrinda insisted.

Drishtant kept quiet for a while. As always, Vrinda was successful in convincing him.

"Are you listening, Drishtant? Call her!" said Vrinda again.

"Okay, I will call her in a while," Drishtant said in a low voice. He had realised his mistake by then.

"No, you talk to her right now and tell her that you are taking her out for dinner tonight."

Drishtant called Lalsa and invited her for dinner.

Lalsa's conscience did not allow her to forgive him for his misbehaviour. Every time, Drishtant fought with Lalsa over small issues to hurt her badly and afterwards showered expensive gifts to compensate. But what he didn't realise was that for Lalsa, her self-esteem and independence were more important than materialistic things. By imposing his will on her, he was slowly and gradually crushing her self confidence. Drishtant treated her as his property; he imposed his decisions on her. She didn't know what to do but ultimately decided to go for dinner and hoped that something would work out between them.

9

A Feather-brained Friend

While things were still unsettled between Drishtant and Lalsa, Shikha introduced Lalsa to her friend, Dimpy. Dimpy was Shikha's old friend. She had a very stylish haircut and liked dressing up. She was a single child, with a father who was a property dealer and a mother who was a homemaker. Her parents were very fond of partying. Her mother enjoyed exhibiting fake branded clothes and bags at parties. Like her mother, Dimpy was also materialistic, crazy about boys and their expensive gifts. Lalsa found her to be chirpy and funny. She always had a lot of gossip to entertain them and Lalsa also enjoyed meeting her occasionally with Shikha.

One day, Dimpy called up Lalsa and Shikha and asked both of them to meet her as she had some exciting news to share with them. They all met at Café Coffee Day. Dimpy seemed super excited.

"Hey girls, guess what? Very soon I am going to be a big star," Dimpy said in an animated voice. Lalsa and Shikha failed to understand the full import of what she had announced.

"Actually my boyfriend, Nitesh, is going to promote me in the fashion industry as a model. He introduced me to his friend who owns a very big advertising agency. They called me for an interview. Now, I am waiting for their response," declared Dimpy to dissolve the suspense she had created.

"Who interviewed you?" Lalsa asked excitedly.

"Nitesh took me to his friend's house who is the owner of an advertising agency. He told me that his agency is looking for a model for a company that manufactures lingerie. He and his team took my interview and the screen test too."

"But what did they ask you?" asked Shikha inquisitively.

"They asked about my body measurements and then told me to walk in my undergarments. I did that. They clicked my pictures and told me that soon they would get back to me."

"But who were they? Did you check their credentials?"

"There were three boys along with my friend, Nitesh."

"Did you ask the name of their agency? Did you inquire about the credentials of the company?"

"No! But Nitesh told me they have an advertising agency."

"Then why did they call you to their residence instead of their office or studio? Oh my god! Without checking anything you just took off your clothes in front of unknown men?" Lalsa was vexed with Dimpy who became visibly uncomfortable and her face turned pale.

"What should I do now? What if they blackmail me then?" Dimpy was scared.

"You call your boyfriend right now and get the details of the company."

"But right now he will be with his father." Dimpy said worriedly.

"Okay, then text him!" Lalsa was determined.

Dimpy texted a message to her boyfriend Nitesh, saying,

"Hi, Nitesh. Please give me the details of the advertising agency which took my interview for modelling"

"Why? Why do you want the details?" Nitesh replied.

"Actually one of my friends is also from the same line. She wants to know the details."

"Don't you trust me? Why do you want to get their credibility authenticated by someone else?"

"It is not like that. I just wanted to know the name of the agency."

"No, I can't give the name of their agency. They are my friends and if they come to know that you are spying on them, they will be hurt. Now I am busy, so don't bother me further."

Lalsa and Shikha were sure by then that Nitesh had misled her. But what should be done to control further damage was the question. They decided to take a stern action against those boys. After contemplating, they decided to take Drishtant's help. They went to Shikha's house and called Drishtant and confided everything in him on the condition that it would be kept a secret. Drishtant scolded them for being careless but ultimately agreed to extend his help to them.

Next day, after college they all met. All of them along with Drishtant went to Nitesh's father's office. They met him and told him everything about the incident and threatened to file an FIR against Nitesh and his friends unless they received a written apology from all of them. Nitesh was summoned and he admitted before his father that he had played a prank on Dimpy. He also admitted that his friends didn't run any advertising agency. His father slapped him in front of everyone and called the other three boys to his office. All of them deleted Dimpy's video from their phones and gave a written apology, admitting their fault. Nitesh's father threatened them that in future if they bothered Dimpy in any way, he himself would report the matter to the police.

Lalsa and her friends were happy about their victory. Dimpy thanked Drishtant. She was sad to know the reality of her boyfriend but was happy to have taught an appropriate lesson to all of them.

10

Do I Love or Hate Him?

It was Shikha's birthday. Her mother had organised a party to celebrate the occasion. All her cousins and close relatives were invited. Lalsa and Shikha bought their dresses from Zara. Lalsa wore a long, red dress, which draped beautifully on her body. She looked sexy and attractive. When she entered the party, no one could stop staring at her. Shikha welcomed her with a hug and mumbled in her ears, "What are your intentions? Want to kill my brother?"

"Yes!" Lalsa answered with a chuckle.

Shikha held her hand and introduced her to the guests. But Lalsa's eyes were desperately searching for Drishtant. She wanted to see appreciation for her in his eyes.

"Where is he?" Lalsa whispered.

"Don't worry, he is coming. My God! Think of the devil and devil is here," Shikha said with a laugh and pointed towards the door.

Drishtant saw her and their eyes met. She saw appreciation in his eyes. But suddenly his expression changed when he saw that she was wearing an off-shouldered dress. He looked furious.

He rushed towards her, took her by the arm and said, "What is this? What are you wearing? Are you mad?"

Lalsa was taken aback.

"What? What happened?" Lalsa spluttered.

"You are looking obnoxious! Go and change your dress immediately."

"But I don't have another dress," Lalsa said.

"You go to Shikha's room and tell her to give you some decent dress to wear."

"No, Drishtant, how is that possible? Everybody has seen me in this dress. How can I change my clothes now? What if somebody asks me why I changed my clothes?" Lalsa resisted.

"Then leave the party and go back home," Drishtant said sternly.

Lalsa held her tears back and proceeded towards the door to leave. At the same time, Shikha's mother saw her going out.

"Where are you going?"

"No no, Aunty! I am not going anywhere," Lalsa lied and returned to the centre of the hall.

Drishtant was watching her with smouldering eyes. He picked up a glass of water and came near her.

"So you don't have an excuse to go?" He asked and threw water on her clothes while pretending to lose his balance.

"Now you can leave. You have a reason," said Drishtant with a sting in his voice.

Lalsa was bewildered. She never knew that he was capable of stooping so low to fulfil his wish. She hatefully looked at him and immediately turned back to leave the hall. The driver was waiting outside. She immediately sat in the car to avoid anyone's attention.

Vrinda saw Lalsa leaving the hall hurriedly. She sensed that something had happened between Drishtant and Lalsa. She immediately caught hold of Drishtant and took him to another room.

"Why did Lalsa leave the party so abruptly? Did you say something to her?" Vrinda asked angrily.

"She knows that I don't like her wearing such clothes. Then why does she offend me every time for the same reason?" Drishtant was fuming with anger.

"She is not offending you. Your own big ego and unreasonable expectation are offending you," Vrinda seemed to be genuinely angry this time.

"What are you saying, Aunty? I don't understand your philosophy. I love her and do so much for her. The least she can do is to respect my sentiments in return."

"Have you struck a business deal with her that if you love her, she should obey each of your commands and lead her life according to your set norms? Is this love? Whenever you decide that she has not acted according to your whims and fancies, your ego gets hurt and you get mad. It is not she but your expectations that are hurting you, Drishtant! Please mend your ways, lower the level of your ego and expectations. Accept her individuality because acceptance is the key to all successful relationships."

"I do so much for her. Can't she adjust this much for a person who loves her madly?" Drishtant protested again.

"What if she asks you the same question? Can't you modify your preferences for her love? I agree you do a lot for her but she doesn't ask or force you for anything. Doing things for her is your own choice, which I am sure must be giving you a lot of pleasure. So please don't expect anything more after that."

"But she should respect my feelings," Drishtant said in a low voice. Vrinda's logic seemed to have cooled him down by then.

"It applies to you also, *beta*! You should also respect her feelings, freedom and individuality. Don't try to stifle her. Her happiness should be the matter of utmost importance to you. Why do you have to hurt her always? Now leave immediately and try to get her back," Vrinda instructed.

"I don't think she will come back."

"Then you should also be with her. She should be more important to you than this party. Go!" Vrinda said with a smile and literally pushed him out of the room.

After she reached home, Lalsa rushed to her bedroom, and cried into her pillow. Luckily, her parents were not at home. About half an hour later, Drishtant called her.

"Lalsa, please open the door, I am standing outside your house."

"No, I don't want to meet you! Go away!"

"Baby, I will go away after you eat your food. I know you must have not eaten anything."

"I am not hungry. I don't want to eat anything."

"But I am very hungry. I didn't have lunch either."

"You go back and have your food at your own house."

"Have mercy on me, please! My stomach is rumbling because of hunger. You know me well. I will not go without meeting you, so please open the door without wasting any time." Drishtant pleaded.

Lalsa didn't want to meet him as she was too hurt to be ready for a truce. But she knew that he would not budge from the door of her house without meeting her. She reluctantly went downstairs and opened the door. Drishtant hugged her warmly.

"I think you are alone. Let's go to your room, I will feed you with my hands." Drishtant said lovingly.

Lalsa was amazed to see him. His face was serene and calm like the still water of the sea after a storm. She wondered if he was the same person who had thrown her out of his house mercilessly just an hour ago. On reaching her room, he hugged her tightly and showered kisses on her face and neck.

"Please stop! I feel stifled." Lalsa was irritated.

"Okay! Now you show me your dress properly," Drishtant said while holding her apart from himself. Taking her arms in his hands he looked at her from top to toe and said, "Oh my god! You look so hot!" He started kissing her shoulders and back amorously. "You are looking so beautiful!" he continued.

"Please stop this and let's eat," Lalsa said.

As Drishtant had said, he fed her with his own hands. That night, he decided never to get mad at Lalsa again.

Alone in her bed that night, Lalsa wondered whether she loved or hated Drishtant.

11

A Cuckold

In the morning, when Lalsa was having breakfast, the landline rang. Her mother picked up the phone and after a moment of silence, she fell on the chair and started yelling. Lalsa and her father left the breakfast table and ran towards her.

"What happened, Kanta?" Vijay asked worriedly.

"*Bhai sahib* is no more! He has committed suicide."

"What?" Vijay was stunned.

"How could he do that?" Vijay said in a hurtful voice. He failed to control his emotions and looked devastated. Helplessly, he sat down on the chair. Kanta placed her hand on his shoulder and said, "Hurry up, we have to reach their house immediately. Lalsa, finish your breakfast and come with us."

All three of them went to Sanjay's house. Upon reaching his house, they found the body on the floor surrounded by all the near and dear ones. Lalsa sat in the corner of the room where a man was standing and sobbing. She recognised him immediately. It was Sanjay uncle's closest friend, Dilip.

At night, when she was trying to sleep, she remembered Dilip. Images from the past that were connected to Dilip started haunting her. Her uncle, Sanjay, was married to her aunt, Asha and they had three sons. Dilip was the closest childhood friend of Sanjay Uncle. Dilip was always seen around Sanjay and Asha. All three of them were almost inseparable but Dilip's wife maintained a distance from all three for reasons no one knew. Dilip didn't have any children. After a few years of marriage, his wife died due to cancer and he was left alone. Thereafter, his proximity with Sanjay and Asha increased further.

Lalsa was fond of her aunt, Asha and her cousins, Amit and Sumit. During the vacations, Lalsa used to visit them frequently and spend a large part of her holidays with them. She clearly remembered the day in Delhi when she was in Class VI, her cousins were at their grandmother's house for two days. Lalsa was feeling bored, so she joined her aunt for a shopping spree.

She took her to a jewellery shop and looked at a couple of expensive diamond earrings. She shortlisted two pairs of earrings and told the shopkeeper that she would come later to buy those pieces. Lalsa was surprised as her uncle was not rich enough to afford expensive diamond jewellery for his wife. When she asked Asha Aunty whether she was buying those earrings for herself, Asha said that her sister wanted Asha to select earrings for her. Lalsa was convinced.

Next day, Lalsa herself wanted to go for shopping, so she went to Asha's place to ask her if she could accompany her. She rang the doorbell. Asha opened the door and looked as if she was in between a meal. She gave Lalsa a weird look as if she had visited her house at the wrong time. She could feel that she was an unwanted guest that day. When she went inside, she saw Dilip sitting and eating *dosa* at the dining table. There was no other plate on the table. Although Lalsa was very young, she was sharp enough to assess that they were eating from the same plate in the absence of her uncle and the pair of earrings which Asha Aunty had selected the other day were adorning her ears. Lalsa felt uncomfortable and left the house immediately. She understood that Dilip must have gifted Asha Aunty those earrings. She wondered whether they were having a clandestine affair!

After a few days, Asha wore the same earrings at a family function. When Kanta admired the earrings, she said that they were her sister's. But Lalsa knew the truth.

One day, Asha took Lalsa with her to the Bhrigu Santa Ashram where she met a saint. She asked him about her future. The saint asked her name and date of birth and searched out few bundles of old yellowish thick papers. He took out one page and started reading. He correctly guessed the first alphabet of her husband's and children's names. Then he predicted that she would lose her husband within a span of five years and the person whose name starts with 'D' would be the reason for his death. Her aunt got angry and started blabbering that such a thing was not possible. The saint snubbed her and said that he was only reading the page of her future. He did not add nor delete anything from the written page. Lalsa got scared on hearing the prediction but she decided to keep it a secret and went back to Mussoorie. By the next vacations, she had almost forgotten the saint's prediction.

During her next vacation, she again went to stay at Asha Aunty's house and was playing cards with her cousins. Asha Aunty was also sitting in the same room and sharing Lalsa's cards. Suddenly, the door bell rang. Her aunt went to see who was at the door. Lalsa and her cousins were busy playing. Meanwhile, Lalsa felt a strong urge to drink water. She went to the kitchen and saw that Dilip held her aunt in an embrace and was trying to kiss her lips. Thankfully, his back was towards Lalsa and her aunt's face was covered with his back, so neither of them noticed her. She immediately went back to the room and pretended as if she had not gone out of the room. She didn't tell anyone about the incident but decided to maintain a distance from her aunt.

Lalsa was told that Sanjay Uncle was suffering from severe depression and was hospitalised. She was sure that Dilip and Asha Aunty were responsible for his untimely death. Her uncle must have found out about their relationship because of which he was depressed and ultimately committed suicide. In her heart, she felt like telling everything to her parents but chose to keep quiet as she was too young to interfere in their family affair. Also, she didn't have any proof to prove her aunt's infidelity. She wondered how true was the prediction made by the Bhrigu saint. She hated her aunt for her misdeeds and vowed in her heart to never talk to her again.

12

A Possessive Lover

Diwali was around the corner and everyone was excited about it. A Diwali party was organised at Shikha's house. Both Shikha and Lalsa decided to wear sari as the dress code was Indian.

Drishtant was also very happy to see her in a sari. He was standing close to her when one of Shikha's cousin who had never met Lalsa earlier, came to meet Drishtant. He stared at Lalsa without blinking his eyes while shaking hands with Drishtant. Drishtant didn't like this at all. He introduced Lalsa as Shikha's friend and immediately held Lalsa's hand as if he was declaring that she was his property.

"Hi, I am Sidharth," the boy introduced himself to Lalsa. "I must compliment you, Lalsa! I have never ever seen a girl more beautiful than you," he continued.

"Thanks!" Lalsa said and looked elsewhere to avoid the wrath of Drishtant.

"Especially your long, beautiful hair. Only Italians have this hair colour. It really compliments you. Have you coloured your hair or is it naturally like this?" Sidharth was not ready to budge from there.

"Yes, it is natural!" Lalsa mumbled fearfully. She could see that Drishtant was getting red under the collar.

"Excuse me!" she said and hurriedly proceeded towards Shikha. The rest of the night passed by peacefully, though Drishtant looked upset till the end of the party. Lalsa deliberately avoided Sidharth's topic. That night, he didn't drop her back home but called her the next morning.

"Hi, Lalsa get ready. I will pick you up at eleven."

"But where are we going? Lalsa was curious. Drishtant didn't answer and hung up. Lalsa got frightened but she controlled herself as she knew that he was upset because of the previous night's incident. She quickly got ready to accompany Drishtant. Drishtant arrived at sharp 11:00 a.m. Lalsa sat in his car and asked, "Where are we going Drishtant?"

"Wait for ten minutes." Drishtant answered rudely.

"Is everything fine?"

Drishtant was not ready to disclose anything. After a while, he stopped his car at a beauty salon.

"Come, we have an appointment for your haircut."

"What? Why? I don't want to cut my hair," Lalsa rebelled.

"But I don't like your long hair. I want you to have a different style. Now get down!" he said persuasively and got down to open the car door for her.

Lalsa didn't move from her seat. "No, I will not go! I love my long hair. My mom will also get shocked if I get my hair cut." she said firmly and freed her hand from his fist.

"You are only concerned about your wish. What about me?" Drishtant said furiously and yanked her out forcefully. She got out of the car with a jerk. Something inside her heart forced her to rebel. She started pummelling him hard with her fist on his chest.

"Let me be! Today you are telling me to cut my hair, tomorrow you may force me to change the colour of my skin. Leave me or I will shout," Lalsa raised her voice.

People started gathering around them. Fear took over Drishtant. Lalsa freed her hand and immediately took a cab to go back home. By then, Drishtant had realised his mistake. He loved her madly, and he could not afford to lose her. He followed her immediately. Lalsa reached home and locked herself in her room. After few minutes, Drishtant also reached her house and the house help opened the door. Lalsa's mother was not at home. Drishtant went upstairs and started banging on the door of her room.

"Lalsa, please open the door. I will never do it again. It was my fault. I promise from now onwards, I will control my self. Please forgive me! Give me at least one more chance."

Lalsa was badly hurt and was too offended to open the door. Drishtant kept pleading. Finally, Lalsa opened the door. As always, they made up but a part of Lalsa's heart was bruised and she needed time to recover.

Drishtant never expected that Lalsa could ever retaliate as he had always seen her milder side. That's why he always took her for granted. But that day, he realised that if he didn't control his behaviour, he could lose her forever. He vowed in his heart to control his possessiveness and anger in future.

13

A Friend Gets Hooked

Drishtant had to go to Mumbai for a few days on business. In his absence, Lalsa enjoyed her freedom. Shikha and Dimpy invited her to accompany them to a popular place called 'Smaaash' in Gurugram. Dimpy had organised the programme. She told Shikha and Lalsa that her new boyfriend and his friends would also be there. Lalsa was a little apprehensive but agreed to join them after a lot of persuasion.

Shikha picked up Lalsa from her house. Both of them got dropped at Connaught Place. Shikha was dressed in a blue dress, and had also curled her hair. Lalsa had never seen her like this.

"What's going on Shikha? Why are you so decked up today? Are you meeting someone?" Lalsa asked laughingly.

"Who knows? I may meet the boy of my dreams. I am fed up of being alone. Every day, Dimpy tells me interesting stories about different boys and I just keep listening like a fool. I feel so belittled. Dimpy told me that her boyfriend's friend, Jatin, the most desirable boy of Delhi, is also joining us today," Shikha said excitedly.

Lalsa burst into a merry laugh.

"Crazy girl! You can't go for hunting a boyfriend. When it is destined to happen, it will happen. Don't let this get you down. My blessings are with you, *baccha*!" Lalsa raised her hand and posed like a saint blessing her followers. Both of them had a hearty laugh. Meanwhile, a car stopped near them.

"Come on girls!" Dimpy shouted from the back seat.

Both of them sat in the car quickly as they didn't want to be seen with the boys. Lalsa and Shikha exchanged pleasantries with everyone. Dimpy and her boyfriend were sitting in the back seat. The boy driving the car was Jatin and the one sitting on the co-driver's seat was Manas. Most of the time, Dimpy and her boyfriend were talking as they were the common link in the group. After an hour, they reached the place. There were lots of options for entertainment like video games, finger coaster, sky-karting, bowling alleys, restaurants, etc. Manas was shy and busy with his mobile all the time while Jatin was chatty. Jatin was incessantly trying to flirt with Lalsa and Shikha. But Lalsa was not ready to entertain him. Shikha, however, was very excited to see that Jatin was showing interest in her. They exchanged phone numbers also.

Shikha quickly became a part of the gang, while Lalsa felt out of place. She wondered why she had agreed to join them. In fact, she missed Drishtant and felt guilty. Drishtant called her twice. She lied to him about where she was and told him that she was shopping with Shikha.

After a while, everyone was quite comfortable with each other. They shared funny and interesting moments of their lives, laughed, commented on each other and very soon the walls of formality came down. Lalsa maintained her distance from everyone as she didn't want to entangle herself with anyone unnecessarily. All of them enjoyed themselves and then decided to eat something and get back home.

Next day, when Shikha met Lalsa, she was super excited. She told Lalsa that last night she and Jatin had talked for a long time over the phone and had planned to go for a drive together in the evening. Lalsa warned her to be careful as it was not safe to go alone so soon with a boy whom she had met only once. But Shikha was not ready to listen. She said that she had discussed this with Dimpy and Dimpy had told her that there was no harm in meeting him alone. Later in the evening, Shikha called Lalsa and told her that Jatin had kissed her. It was a very special and a beautiful experience for her as it was the first kiss of her life.

Days passed by and in spite of Lalsa's warning, Shikha got very close to Jatin both physically and emotionally. Shikha introduced Jatin to her mother also. Jatin belonged to an affluent family and was very courteous towards her mother, so Vrinda liked him and was open to their relationship. Shikha was upset as her parents were planning a trip to Bangkok to celebrate her mother's fiftieth birthday. They wanted her to join them. Shikha didn't want to go as she was mentally too engrossed with Jatin but couldn't say no to her parents. With only two days left for their departure, her father had to excuse himself from the trip because of a business compulsion. Shikha and her mother left for Bangkok, and Shikha asked Jatin to join them secretly to which he agreed. She was extremely thrilled to spend a holiday with him in Bangkok.

When Shikha returned from the trip, she shared a horrifying incident with Lalsa that happened while she was in Bangkok. She told Lalsa that Jatin met them in Bangkok and pretended as if he had been there for a business meeting.

Shikha's mother didn't believe him but pretended to be convinced. The first two days with him were very good. They went sightseeing, and for dinners and excursions together. Jatin was extra caring towards her mother because of which her mother was also quite impressed by him.

On the third day, Shikha and Jatin decided to go for a body massage in the massage parlour of the hotel. Shikha went to the ladies massage room and Jatin went to the men's massage room. When Shikha returned to her room, she found her mother packing the luggage.

"What are you doing, Mom? Why are you packing right now? We have to go back day after tomorrow."

"You also pack your baggage immediately. We are not going to stay in this hotel with that bastard." Vrinda was extremely furious.

"Mom, who are you talking about?"

"Who else…your friend Jatin," Vrinda was livid.

"Jatin! What are you saying, Mom?"

"Yes, Jatin. He came to my room about half an hour ago. I offered to make coffee for him. When I was making coffee for him, he hugged me from behind and said, 'You are so sweet. I really love you.'

"I was taken aback but giving him the benefit of doubt, I said that I also liked him as he is like my son, and freed myself from his arms."

'You are more beautiful than Shikha,' he said. I tried to change the topic and asked him if he would like to have something with coffee.

'I only need your love,' he answered with a nasty smile. His face had turned red and it was evident that he was drunk; his body language clearly showed his intentions. I politely told him to go to his room but he refused to leave."

'No, I will not go like this,' he insisted and then tried to kiss me. I pushed him out of the room and locked myself from inside.

Shikha was crestfallen after hearing the whole story. She felt highly ashamed to hear the incident narrated by her mother and didn't know how to react. She wanted to give Jatin a tight slap but her mother stopped her. They moved to another hotel immediately and after that, Shikha didn't talk to Jatin. They all returned by the same flight because of prior bookings but avoided each other completely.

Lalsa was surprised to hear her story. She wondered how Jatin could stoop so low that he tried to make love to the mother of the girl he was in a relationship with.

14

Jealous Baby

It was the last week of December and only two days were to the New Year. Drishtant and his cousins decided to celebrate New Year's Eve together at Ashoka Hotel. Shikha and Lalsa also accompanied them. Together, as a group they went to celebrate the night. All of them were excited about the fun they would have. Everyone tried to look their best as there were titles such as 'best-looking boy' and 'best-looking girl'. Lalsa wore a long black dress and complemented it with a beautiful string of pearls.

The night was sparkling. There were different kinds of performances. To start with, there was a group of belly dancers who entertained the guests. Everybody was enjoying the evening with drinks, food and music. After some performances, everyone was invited to the dance floor. Drishtant and Lalsa also went to the floor and danced closely with each other. They kept dancing till midnight. Suddenly, all the lights were turned off and the countdown began for the last sixty seconds of the year. Drishtant and Lalsa kissed each other for the first second of the New Year.

The result for the 'best-looking boy and girl' was declared. Lalsa won the title of the most beautiful girl.

Everyone at their table was very happy and so was Drishtant. The title winners were invited on the stage. The boy shook hands with her enthusiastically.

"Hi, I am Nishant. Congratulations! You are really very beautiful." Then he put his arm around Lalsa's shoulder for a photograph. Lalsa didn't like him getting close to her.

"I would love to meet you again. This is my card. I will wait for your call." He said quickly and handed over his visiting card to Lalsa who was stunned by his confidence. Everything happened so quickly that she couldn't even react. After he left, she tried to see Drishtant but the table where he was sitting along with his cousins was at a distance. She could not see Drishtant clearly. But all his cousins were clapping continuously and cheering her. She immediately threw Nishant's card away and rushed to her table.

One look at Drishtant's face and she realised that the storm was not too far. Everyone hugged her and congratulated her but she was fraught with fear because of the expression on Drishtant's face. Only few minutes back, Drishtant was very vibrant but now he was quiet and seemed disinterested in everything. Everyone had food but Drishtant skipped dinner saying that he was too full because of snacks and booze. Lalsa either didn't eat anything as she was expecting Drishtant to explode with rage anytime now.

Drishtant was supposed to drop Lalsa back home. Lalsa thought that he would start scolding her as soon as he got a chance but to her surprise, he didn't utter a word. He was trying his level best to control his anger which was very difficult for him but he had promised himself to never get mad at Lalsa. She asked him the reason for his reticence but he didn't answer and dropped her back home. Before getting out of the car, Lalsa wished him good night but again he didn't answer and left.

Next day, he didn't meet her nor did he take her call. Lalsa was very upset. Finally, she decided to go to his office. Luckily he was sitting alone.

"Hi, Drishtant!" Lalsa said smilingly. She knew she would have to make an effort but she felt happy as it was the first time when he had suppressed his anger and checked himself from reacting sharply. He didn't answer and pretended to be engrossed in the file in front of him. Lalsa liked his new avatar. She sat in front of him to catch his gaze but Drishtant ignored her completely. His childish behaviour amused her. She laughed loudly and said,"Oh my god! You are so angry! At least look at me! See I am wearing your favourite dress which you gifted me last week." Lalsa was thoroughly enjoying herself while teasing him but Drishtant didn't budge. She got up, went behind his chair and with both her arms encircled his neck. Then she kissed his cheek.

"Look at me, darling!"

"Show all this to the boy who was flirting with you," ultimately Drishtant expressed his annoyance politely. Lalsa burst into an exuberant laugh. She loved his sober behaviour.

"Oh my jealous, baby! You know nobody matters to me except you. You are my love, my life! I can't live without you, darling." She passionately rubbed her cheeks with his cheeks and kissed his forehead. Drishtant couldn't hold himself back anymore and kissed her. Drishtant enjoyed Lalsa's attention. He was happy that he was finally able to control his anger.

Drishtant had to go out of town on a business trip for three days. It was late in the evening when there was a beep on Lalsa's mobile phone. She received an email that read–

"Can you please call me on the following number?

Waiting,

Robin"

She was excited and confused too. She didn't know whether it was her friend Robin or someone else. Ultimately, she decided to call.

"Hi!"

"Is this you, Robin? Where did you disappear?"

Robin laughed and said, "Yes! It is Robin. Thanks for recognising me in one go. Was I the one who disappeared or you who just vanished? You know the only means of our communication was your number and you changed that also. At least you should have apprised me of your new number. I didn't know how to contact you and then luckily I met Sanya in London who had your email ID."

"Oh you met her? Why didn't she call me?" Lalsa was excited to hear about Sanya after so long.

"She is very annoyed with you because you changed your number without informing her," Robin answered.

Lalsa realised that he was right because her mobile had fallen down in the toilet and stopped working. Drishtant had gifted her a new mobile phone with a new SIM card after which she had discarded the old phone and lost all the old phone numbers.

"I am sorry, Robin. Actually, I had not memorised anybody's number. These were fed in my mobile which fell down in the toilet. I lost all my old contacts."

"Okay, Lalsa! I can't wait to see you! Can we meet tomorrow? I have especially come from London especially to see you."

Lalsa was so excited to talk to Robin that her relationship with Drishtant completely slipped out of her mind. But when

Robin asked her to meet, she didn't know what else to say as she was very scared of Drishtant and his possessiveness. Now, she felt it would be rude to not meet him, since they had spent some beautiful moments together and Robin had come to Delhi just to see her.

Still she was confused. To gain some time in order to take the right decision, she said, "Okay, Robin give me some time. I will call you back."

"But promise me that you will meet me."

Lalsa kept quiet for a while then said, "Don't worry! I will call you tomorrow morning and let you know," and then disconnected the phone.

Lalsa was both nervous and excited to meet Robin. She slipped into the reminiscences of her schooldays when she had met Robin for the first time.

15

Old Flame

Lalsa walked past the memory lane of her Class XII. The annual carnival, the most-happening and most-awaited event of Lalsa's school was around the corner. Another branch of their school in Mussoorie was exclusively for the boys. Every year, the annual carnival was held at the boy's school where students of the girl's branch were also invited to participate. The event was called 'Socials'. Since it was the only occasion where the boys and the girls could interact with each other without any restrictions, everyone looked forward to it. The girls and the boys would start planning their dresses, performances and everything much before the event.

Finally, the day arrived and Lalsa wore a white gown and curled her long brown hair. She looked beautiful and everyone's eyes were on her.

A number of stalls were put up in the school playground. In the stadium, several competitions were held amongst boys and girls. Sanya stood first in the light music competition. Lalsa walked on the ramp and won the title of the prettiest girl.

The assembly room was converted into a disco where anybody could dance after paying the entry fee. Lalsa was very fond of dancing, she and her friends headed towards the dance floor. While they were dancing, one of the boys dared the girls to compete with their best dancer, Robin who was an extraordinary dancer. All the girls coaxed Lalsa to accept the challenge as they were confident of her dancing skills.

Robin and Lalsa did a dance, both showcased their dance moves and finally, Lalsa won the challenge. Robin gave up but by the end, he was completely smitten by Lalsa. He tried to be friendly with Lalsa but she ignored him. Lalsa's friends also noticed Robin's fascination and began to tease her.

A week passed by. On a Sunday afternoon, Lalsa was informed that there was a visitor for her in the visitor's lounge. To her surprise, it was Robin with a bouquet of flowers in his hands. Both of them exchanged pleasantries. Lalsa had never imagined in her wildest dream that Robin would come to see her. She didn't have any feelings for him. In fact, she was annoyed with him, as she had to face embarrassment because of him. Even Sister Louisa had told her to be wary of the boys after learning of Robin's interest in her. She had got scared to see him in the school and had wanted to send him back as soon as possible. While Lalsa was in a whirlpool of emotions, he presented her the bouquet.

"What should I do with it? My friends are already teasing me because of your behaviour that day."

"I am extremely sorry for that but I couldn't stop myself because you were looking so pretty," said Robin.

"But I don't like it and please take these flowers back."

Lalsa was in no mood to acknowledge his appreciation.

"Okay, I will take these flowers back but please don't get annoyed."

"Please don't come here again, as I don't want any controversy."

"Okay! Sorry I bothered you unnecessarily," Robin said disappointedly. He picked up the bouquet from the table and immediately left the room.

Lalsa was taken aback as she did not expect him to leave abruptly. She wondered if she had treated him harshly unnecessarily. Somewhere in her heart, she felt guilty and confided in Sanya, who further aggravated her guilt by saying that there was no need to be so rude with Robin. On the contrary, she appreciated Robin's behaviour and said that both of them looked a perfect pair on the dance floor. At night, while trying to sleep Lalsa kept thinking about Robin. She wished to see him again and make up for her misbehaviour.

About a month later, her mother came to spend a weekend with her. As usual, they went to her favourite restaurant to have lunch, after which Lalsa wanted to eat ice cream. Since, her mother was not very keen on eating it, Lalsa went to the ice cream parlour by herself. When Lalsa reached the parlour, she saw Robin buying ice cream from there. Robin saw her and his eyes twinkled instantly with joy but soon he controlled his emotions and wished her in a very low voice. Lalsa also felt good to see him. In fact, after snubbing him in their last meeting, she had been feeling guilty.

"Hi! How are you, Robin? It has been long since I heard from you. Hope you are fine!" She said it all in one breath as she wanted to make up for her rude behaviour. Robin was amazed to note a change in her tone. He didn't know how to react. He didn't expect such an overwhelming response from her ever.

"I am good! How is it that you are here? I thought you were not allowed to go out of the school hostel without your guardian. "

"Yes, my mother has come to spend the weekend with me. She was tired after having lunch. I wanted to eat ice cream and spend some more time on Mall Road," Lalsa said.

"You are right! It is so refreshing being on Mall Road. If you want, I can give you company," Robin said happily.

"I don't mind!"

They sat on a bench on the roadside. They talked about their families. Robin was a single child. His mother was an English woman and his father was an Indian. He started his career as a manager in an Indian handicraft export house. After a few years, he left the job to start a small manufacturing unit of handicrafts with four of his colleagues. They started supplying their products to the export houses and gradually started exporting their products directly to the big stores of Europe. His mother was working in a marketing wing of a multinational company in London where his father met her. Despite their cultural differences and resistance from their families, they chose each other as their life partners. Since, his parents had to travel frequently, Robin was sent to boarding school.

Lalsa was curiously listening about his family. Both of them enjoyed each other's company. They were so busy talking that Lalsa did not realise the time. It had been an hour and a half, and Lalsa was anxious about her mother. She decided to take a rickshaw and promised Robin to meet him again the next day.

When she reached the hotel, she was relieved to find that the room was bolted and her mother was sleeping. After meeting Robin, Lalsa's opinion of him changed. She found him to be a very soft spoken, cultured and a sophisticated boy. In fact, she was looking forward to meeting him again but wondered what reason she should give her mother to go alone the next day. Meanwhile, her mother woke up.

"When did you come, dear?"

"It has been quite some time now, Mom. You were sleeping and I thought that I should not disturb you." Lalsa lied to her mother and she knew that she would have to lie again the next day to meet Robin.

"Should I make tea for you?" she said to change the topic.

"Okay, dear!" said her mother."

"Are you okay, Mom? You look exhausted. Is everything fine? How is Dad?"

"Everything is fine but I worry about your father because he has to travel very frequently out of Delhi. I keep worrying about his health. His health is deteriorating. I feel very lonely without him. Very often, I feel that I should shift to Mussoorie. In that case, at least you will be with me. But then I can't leave your father alone."

Lalsa listened to her mother patiently and said,"Why don't you tell Sanjay Uncle to talk to Dad about this issue?"

"I requested Sanjay *bhaiya* to talk to your dad. He told me that he would come and talk to him personally but he didn't come. I don't know what has happened to him, he doesn't go anywhere now."

"But why don't you tell Dad to take it easy. Tell him to slow down and take care of his health. "

"I keep telling him but he doesn't listen to me. There are times when we pick up a fight because of this. "

"But Mom, you are such an understanding person, even if he doesn't listen to you, don't give him and yourself extra stress by fighting. Whenever he is with you, try to enjoy that time and be happy."

"I try to be calm but fail when after every two to three days, he tells me that he is going for a business trip again. But you are right, I should try harder to not quarrel with him. Anyway, what is your programme now? Do you want to go out for dinner or should we order something?"

"Mom, I want to relax in your lap and watch television after which we will order something," Lalsa said and switched on the TV. Both mother and daughter chatted and watched TV till late into the night. Before sleeping, Lalsa had already figured out how to go alone to meet Robin the next day.

Next morning, after she finished breakfast, Lalsa told her mother that she would have to go out for sometime as it was her friend's birthday, and that the friend had invited a small group for lunch in town. Her mother was a little disappointed. However, she gave her permission to go but on one condition–to return on time. Lalsa called Robin to meet her at 1:00 p.m. at the end of Mall Road at the police check post. When Lalsa reached the meeting point, she saw Robin waiting for her in his car. He was driving the car himself. Lalsa sat next to him and both of them drove off to Lal Tibba. It was a cloudy day which Lalsa had always loved. She always felt that Mussoorie looked much better, greener and romantic under a cloudy sky.

Going for a drive with a partner of her own choice through the beautiful valley covered with clouds, was a thrilling experience for Lalsa. She was thoroughly enjoying the nature. The previous night's thunderstorm and heavy rainfall had left the trees with weak branches and leaves. The branches had bent down after the strong thrashing of the storm and the ruthless rain of the previous night. On the contrary, strong trees with thick branches and leaves looked brighter and stood straight with pride like winners. Suddenly, all the trees hid behind a thick layer of white and grey clouds but after a while the trees came out of the camouflage when the clouds travelled ahead. It seemed as if they were playing hide and seek with the universe.

Robin played a CD of beautiful romantic numbers. She couldn't have asked for more on the first date of her life. They had lunch at a restaurant and then went to Lal Tibba point for a breathtaking view of the valley. No wonder Mussoorie is called 'The Queen of Hill Stations' they realised. While returning, they stopped at Chaar Dukaan to have tea and waffles. They shared a lot about themselves, their friends, teachers and interesting experiences of their lives. They were very comfortable with each other as if they knew each other for long. While the car came down the valley, Robin held her hand. His soft and warm hand gave her a very soothing feeling. It was the first time any boy had held her hand like that.

"Please meet me tomorrow, because then your mother will go away and we will not be able to meet for long," Robin requested.

"Robin, my mother will leave soon after having lunch tomorrow and drop me back at the school hostel, so it will not be possible to meet you tomorrow."

"But you can come out for an early morning walk. I am sure your mother will not be interested to join you."

"No, she will not join me as she has a knee problem. I think that is a doable. I will meet you early in the morning and then we can go up to Camel Back Road."

Robin hugged her with joy.

"Thank you so much," said Robin while kissing her hand. Suddenly, he realised that he was crossing the line and Lalsa may get offended.

"Sorry!"

Lalsa smiled. Robin felt relieved. He dropped her at the same point from where he had picked her up. When she reached the hotel, she saw her mother standing at the gate.

"What happened? Why did you take so long?" her mother asked worriedly.

"Relax Mom! Everything is fine. Let's go to Mall Road for coffee. Did you talk to Dad today? Tell him to come next week," Lalsa tried to change the topic.

"He doesn't have time for anyone. Why don't you talk to him yourself?"

"I will do that," Lalsa said and smiled as she had successfully diverted her mother's attention elsewhere. After having coffee, they went to Tibetan market for shopping. Both of them remained at Mall Road till late evening, and after having heavy snacks, they returned to the hotel. Lalsa's favourite place for lying down was her mother's lap where she lay down her head to relax. As always, her mother started massaging her head softly with the tip of the fingers of one hand and held Lalsa's hand with another hand. While watching television, Lalsa kept playing with and kissing her mother's hand. She was well acquainted with the contours and each line of her mother's hand.

Next morning, Lalsa got up early to meet Robin. Her mother was sleeping till then but got disturbed because of Lalsa's movement in the room.

"What happened, Lalsa? What are you doing?" her mother asked lazily with her eyes closed.

"Ma, I am just going for a stroll. You relax! I will be back before long," Lalsa said while tying the laces of her sport shoes.

"But why did you get up so soon?"

"Mom, once you leave, I will again be locked up in the hostel which is not less than a jail, so let me enjoy my freedom for some more time."

"Okay, be back soon," her mother said and turned to the other side to resume her sleep.

Robin was standing near the main gate of the hotel. They held hands and walked towards Camel Back. On their way back, it started drizzling. They took shelter under one shed. Robin bought tea from a nearby stall and they sat on a bench. The view was beautiful. The wind was blowing and the leaves were fluttering, the weather was pleasant and so was the company. The trees started swaying gently and delicately like a group of dancers swaying from side to side, holding each other at the waist. A sudden shower stopped their dance for a while like a mother who sometimes stops her children from playing to give them a bath and make them brighter, more beautiful and fresh.

Both of them were quiet and sad. They had run out of words. While they were still sitting there in silence, Robin took out a mobile phone from his jacket.

"Lalsa, it will be very difficult for me to live without talking to you everyday. Therefore, you keep this mobile with you."

"But we are not allowed to keep mobile phones in the hostel."

"I am aware of that. But hide it somewhere and call me whenever you get a chance to talk. I will be waiting every minute to hear from you."

"Okay!"

Robin looked at her. He could not hold back his emotions. He hugged her and said, "I will miss you."

"Me too!" said Lalsa. Both of them walked back towards the hotel and then parted back ways. After they finished breakfast, her mother dropped her back at the school and left for Delhi.

16

The Warmth of Love

After dinner, Sanya and Lalsa went to the school ground for a walk. She shared everything about Robin with Sanya who was very excited and happy to hear her story. They decided to keep it a secret and not share it with anyone else. Lalsa did not sleep well that night. She was not able to come out of the moments spent with Robin. His touch was very precious for her. No boy had ever hugged or touched her. Robin was the first boy who had touched her. She was dying to meet him again.

A month passed by. Robin and Lalsa talked to each other every day on mobile phone. They were getting desperate to meet again but didn't know what to do. Lalsa called her father and insisted that he should come to Mussoorie immediately, saying that she was missing him. She knew that her father would never say no to her.

Her father had spoilt her and had always bowed down to all her reasonable and unreasonable demands. Her mother would object sometimes but her father never listened. Whatever Lalsa said or demanded was the last word for him. She was considered to be a lucky charm whose arrival had brought wealth and prosperity to their house. Therefore, whenever she was at home, her father would see her face before leaving the house for good luck. She was sure that her father would never turn down her demand.

Vijay was astonished at her persistence. She had never insisted to such an extent to come to Mussoorie. Although he had a busy schedule that week but he couldn't say no to her and decided to see her during the weekend. Vijay reached Mussoorie on Saturday afternoon. He told Lalsa not to have lunch at school as he wanted to take her out. Then he picked her up from the school.

Vijay hugged her and asked, "Hey Lalsa, were you really missing me or you need something from me?"

Lalsa's face turned red as she was caught off guard.

"No, Dad! I was really missing you."

"Hmmm!" Vijay said sadly because deep down his heart, he never wanted her daughter to stay away from him.

"Okay then! You must be hungry by now. Let's eat something."

They went to a restaurant for lunch. After reaching the restaurant, Lalsa went to the washroom immediately and called Robin. She told him that she was having lunch with her father at a restaurant near the school and would try to meet him alone for sometime.

She had hardly eaten the food, when she saw Robin enter the same restaurant. Her heart jumped with joy. She was thrilled to see him unexpectedly. He ordered food and sat at the table from where he could see her properly. Lalsa found it difficult to eat as Robin had fixed his gaze on her. She wanted to finish the food quickly and meet him as soon as possible.

After they finished the food, Lalsa and her father reached the hotel. Her father wanted to rest for a while since he had started early in the morning from Delhi. Lalsa told her father that she wanted to go to the market. After coming out of the hotel, she immediately called Robin and told him that she was coming to meet him. Robin had not gone back to his flat and was waiting for her on Mall Road.

Her heart was racing as she walked fast to meet Robin. From the opposite side, Robin was proceeding towards her. He was almost running. Finally, they were right in front of each other. Both were gasping for breath. They wanted to hug each other but controlled themselves and decided to sit in a coffee shop.

"Lalsa, you can't even imagine how difficult it was to wait for you for so many days. I really missed you," Robin said as he held her hand.

"Same here, Robin."

"What is your programme for tomorrow?" Robin asked after a pause.

"My father is going tomorrow after breakfast as he has some urgent work in Delhi. I think it will be difficult for me to see you tomorrow. Not even for a morning walk because if I say that I am going for a walk, then he would be very keen to join me," Lalsa said in a disappointed tone.

"No, no! You can't do this to me. We will have to find some way out. I will make some plan and will let you know by tonight. Before sleeping just check my message."

"Okay!"

She left early and also bought some books from the market as it was not an easy task to fool her father. The whole evening, father and daughter spent a hearty time together. Before sleeping, Lalsa went to the washroom to check Robin's message on the phone. She jumped with joy as Robin had suggested a solid plan to meet. She clicked a selfie from her mobile and sent it to Robin along with the number of her hotel room.

"Lalsa, I will start immediately after breakfast," Vijay informed Lalsa.

"Why, Dad?"

"Because my car is also old like me, so it is better to travel during the day time," Vijay said with a laugh.

"No, Dad you are still so young and handsome." Lalsa said fondly and hugged her father affectionately.

In the morning, when Lalsa finished her breakfast, her father told her to pack her luggage as he wanted to drop her to school hostel before leaving for Delhi. Lalsa told him that one of her friends who was a day-scholar was coming to pick her up. She would spend some time with her after which she would drop her back to the school in her car.

"I hope you are not talking about a boyfriend, right?" said Vijay with a naughty smile.

"Of course not, Dad!"

"I am your best buddy, so tell me do you have a boyfriend?"

"No, Dad. For your kind information I am studying in a girls' school which is no less than a prison. Where would I find a boy?" Lalsa lied.

"Okay! Okay! I was just kidding," Vijay chuckled and hugged her. Suddenly, there was a knock on the door of the room. His father opened the door. A girl Lalsa's age was standing there with a smile.

"Good morning, Uncle! I am Lalsa's friend, Reema," she said.

"Yes, yes! Please come in!" Reema came inside the room, and shook hands with Lalsa.

"Hi, Lalsa!"

"Hi!" Lalsa answered with a smile. She had never seen this girl who was pretending to be her friend. She was Robin's friend's sister, who had come to take her out on Robin's instructions. Lalsa had sent her selfie to Robin, so that she could recognise her easily.

Lalsa's father dropped them on the road as suggested by Reema. She invited Vijay to her house but he declined her offer as he had to leave for Delhi.

"Thank you so much, Reema!" Lalsa expressed her gratitude.

"My pleasure, dear! Come with me."

"But where are we going?"

"I will drop you at Robin's house which is just there." Reema pointed out to an apartment which was on the same road where they were standing. Robin was standing at the door to greet her. He was beaming with joy and excitement on the success of their plan. Reema left immediately after dropping Lalsa.

Lalsa looked around. It was a two room, well-organised flat. Robin held both her hands and said, "Thank God! Nothing went wrong and we succeeded in meeting."

"Yes! I never expected it to happen so smoothly. Everything was just perfect and Reema did an excellent job. By the way, where is your house help?"

"I asked him to come in the evening, since there was not much for him to do today," Robin smiled.

"Okay, tell me should I order something for you?" Robin asked.

"No, not now. I just had my breakfast."

Lalsa and Robin sat on the sofa. Robin picked up the photo album lying on the centre table. "Okay, let me introduce my family to you through the family album." For every photo, he had a story to tell. Lalsa could sense that he was very attached to his parents. She was thoroughly enjoying his company as he was a very talkative and an entertaining person. They chatted for long. Whenever his hand touched Lalsa, she could feel a strange sensation flow through her body. They called for food from the local restaurant. After lunch, Lalsa wanted to go back. Both were sad and didn't want to separate from each other. Lalsa told him to call Reema again to drop her back to the school hostel. Robin hugged her tight and planted a kiss on her forehead.

"Lalsa, both of us are in Class XII and after three months, we will finish school. How will we meet?"

"Don't worry, I will follow you to London!"

"What do you mean?"

"No, I am not lying."

"But how?" Robin asked as it was difficult for him to believe what he had heard.

Lalsa had a hearty laugh.

"Well, you see I want to join London School of Fashion Designing and you will also be in London."

"Wow! That is a very pleasant surprise. You have relieved me from a sense of gloom and insecurity." Robin was very happy and so was Lalsa. Lalsa and Sanya both had dreamt of joining London College of Fashion Designing together.

"When do we meet again? Can I come to see you in your school?" Robin held her hand.

"No, no! Everybody knows you very well. You can't come to my school. Let me try to find another way to meet you soon!"

Robin and Reema dropped her off at the school. Lalsa was very sad that night, missing Robin and longing to meet him again.

The final exams of Class XII were approaching. Robin and Lalsa promised each other to pay more attention to their exams. Both of them were working very hard. Robin kept sending her cards and flowers by the name of Reema. One day, prior to her exams, she received a beautiful pen set with a bouquet of flowers. Lalsa wrote all her exams with the same pens. They talked twice a day during their exams, first to wish each other and then, to know about each other's performance.

It was the evening of their last exam. All the students had planned a party that night. Next day, Lalsa's mother was supposed to come to Mussoorie to take her back from the hostel. She was very happy as she had convinced her mother to stay for a few days in Mussoorie before leaving for Delhi. Robin and Lalsa had decided to make the most of their time together before leaving for Delhi. Robin had promised her that he would follow her to Delhi and stay there for a few days before going to London. Nobody in the hostel wanted to sleep that night. Before joining the party, Lalsa went to the washroom to talk to Robin. She saw five missed calls from Robin on the phone. It was 7:00 p.m. when Lalsa called up Robin.

"Lalsa, where were you? I called you so many times," Robin sounded very upset.

"You know, Robin that I switch off my phone so that no one knows I have one. But what happened?"

"Lalsa, my father has passed away after a cardiac arrest!" Robin was sobbing.

"Oh my god! When? Where?"

"Today, early morning in London. My mother didn't tell me fearing that it would affect my performance in exams.

Now, everybody is waiting there for me to perform the last rites. I am flying tonight itself."

"Oh God! Take care of yourself and your mother and call me after you reach London."

"Okay! I will do that!" Lalsa felt miserable thinking that she would not be able to meet Robin.

It was the last night at the hostel for the students of Class XII. They sang, danced and had a lot of fun. Their teachers also joined them for a while. At 4:00 a.m. in the morning, everyone decided to sleep. Lalsa didn't enjoy herself at all. She talked to Robin twice while he was going to Delhi to catch an early morning flight for London. Robin was completely shattered. On the one hand, he had lost his father and on the other, he was going away from Lalsa, not knowing anything about the future of their relationship.

Everyone slept but Lalsa was very restless. When she called Robin, he had reached Delhi airport and was checking in. They promised to be in touch and meet each other as soon as possible.

Next morning, the students of Class XII were leaving the hostel and Lalsa was expecting her mother to arrive. Her mother was unwell, so she had sent the driver to pick Lalsa. She left Mussoorie with a heavy heart, taking along all the memories of the past nine years in this beautiful city.

After reaching home, everyone kept her so busy with their heart warming welcome that she almost forgot about Robin. When Lalsa was all by herself that night, she decided to text him and typed, "*Hi!*"

After some time, she received Robin's message: "*Hi! I have reached safely. Busy right now. I will contact you later.*"

A week went by but Robin didn't call her back. She missed him every day and was worried about him. Finally, her phone beeped and she got a message from Robin to call him whenever possible. She immediately called him.

"Hi, Robin! How are you and where have you disappeared?"

"I am fine Lalsa. Actually my mom is not well. She had to be hospitalised and I had to be with her all the time. It has been a tough time for all of us, especially her. She is not ready to accept the sudden death of my father. You know, at the time of his death, they were having coffee together. My father had picked a piece of cake to put in his mouth but before taking a bite, he collapsed."

"How is she now?"

"She is better now. I have come home to take my stuff to the hospital. I will be busy again with my mother for next few days. But will call you again as soon as possible."

"Okay! Take care, Robin!" Lalsa said sadly. But Robin was mentally too occupied to notice her sadness. After that, Robin never called her. In her heart, she always felt abandoned by Robin. She had never expected that a person like Robin who seemed to be very sensitive could ignore her completely. She decided to get over him and move on. After getting intensely involved with Drishtant, she had completely forgotten about Robin.

She was confused about meeting him once again. But her heart was not allowing her to shun Robin away ruthlessly. He had come back especially from London to see her. He deserved at least one meeting with her. In the morning, when Robin called her again she told him to meet her at noon.

17

He is a Gentleman

When Lalsa opened her wardrobe to change her clothes and get ready to meet Robin, she was shocked to notice that her whole wardrobe was full of clothes gifted by Drishtant, as he wanted her to wear only those clothes which he bought for her. She felt guilty and sat down on her bed. She wondered whether she was cheating on Drishtant? Should she meet Robin without taking his permission? She knew that if she asked Drishtant, he would never permit her to meet Robin but not meeting Robin would also be very unfair on her part.

She didn't want to cheat on Drishtant. She decided to first meet Robin and later tell everything about him to Drishtant. She knew that Drishtant would be very angry with her but she was ready to bear the wrath of Drishtant for Robin's sake. He deserved at least one last meeting with her. She took out one of her old dresses from the cupboard and got ready to meet Robin. They met in a restaurant. Robin reached the restaurant earlier than Lalsa. When Lalsa reached the table, he stood up and pulled out a chair for her.

"Thanks for meeting me at such a short notice," Robin said with gratitude. He looked more mature. Lalsa smiled and sat down in front of him.

"How have you been, Lalsa? We're meeting after so long!"

"I am absolutely fine, but what happened to you? Why did you disappear? Why did you stop calling me?"

"Lalsa, you don't know, I have been through the hell. My mother sank into severe depression. She became so insecure that it was difficult for me to even go to the washroom. She would not leave my hand even while sleeping. I was the only one to look after her and manage the business. I missed you a lot but could not call you because of my circumstances. Believe me, Lalsa, there was not even a single night when I didn't cry thinking of you." Robin said with moist eyes. He took out his handkerchief and wiped his eyes hurriedly.

"By the time my circumstances improved, you had already changed your phone number and didn't even inform me. I didn't know how to contact you. I tried to find you on Facebook but could not find your account. I went to the London College of Fashion Designing because you told me that you would take admission there, but you were not there. Luckily, I met Sanya there, who gave me your email ID. She was also very angry with you for not contacting her. But now I have her London mobile number, so if you want, you can contact her."

"I am sorry, Robin! I was unnecessarily angry with you without realising that I had changed my number. Please give me Sanya's number also." Lalsa really wanted to talk to her as soon as possible.

"Tell me, what should I order for you?" Robin tried to change the topic.

Lalsa was touched to see his love for her. She was feeling guilty in her heart. She didn't know how to tell him about Drishtant.

"I will have cold coffee. How is your mother now?" she asked.

"She is much better. She has rejoined the business and has also started socialising."

"This is good news."

After that, Lalsa and Robin talked for about half an hour. Lalsa told him about Delhi, her college, her daily routine, but couldn't gather courage to talk about Drishtant. Robin told her that he was doing his graduation in Finance in London and was helping his mother with the business as well.

"Look, how our plans were shattered in a single night. My parents wanted me to go to America for higher studies but I wanted to pursue my studies in London just to be with you. Destiny had its own plans. It cast us away from each other. I couldn't even talk to you. But don't worry now. I will try to come at least once in two months as I have to regularly procure stuff for my store from India."

Lalsa didn't want Robin to express his emotional feelings towards her anymore, therefore, she decided to tell him the truth about Drishtant.

"Yes, Robin that will be very nice but I wanted to tell you something."

"Please tell me what you want to share."

"Robin, please don't get disheartened but..." Lalsa stopped for a while and then gathered courage and said, "I am sorry to say but there is someone else in my life now and I am committed to him."

Robin was stunned. With a fake smile, he said, "I don't believe that! I think you are pulling my leg."

"No, Robin I am telling you the truth!" Lalsa avoided eye contact with him.

"How is that possible Lalsa? Just in a span of a few months, you just got over me, found a new guy and got committed to him?"

Lalsa didn't answer as she was feeling guilty.

"But why, Lalsa? Why didn't you wait for me?"

"Robin, our relationship was very brief after which you just disappeared and did not call me even once. I didn't even know which corner of the world you were in. I thought maybe it was just an infatuation which normally happens in the teenage years and fades away with time."

"I know it is my fault that I completely ignored you, but you know I am a very emotional person and too attached to my mother. She was in such a deplorable condition that I couldn't think about anything else except her well-being. I was so sure about you. I never knew that you would replace me with someone else so soon. When she started recovering, I tried every possible way to get through to you."

"I am sorry, Robin. But can't we just be good friends forever?" Lalsa was embarrassed as she realised her fault. Therefore, she tried to change the topic. He looked at her, paused for a while and with a fake smile he said,"Yes, sure! Actually, I have to leave soon as I have an urgent business meeting," Robin said and called for the bill. For the next ten minutes, till Robin paid the bill, the situation was very awkward for both of them. Suddenly, they felt as if they were strangers. After clearing the bill, Robin left hurriedly. Lalsa sat there for a while with a heavy heart. She had never met such a fine boy in her life. She knew that Robin was hurt very badly and wondered whether he would ever talk to her again.

18

Love Gets Possessive

When Lalsa got up from her seat to come out of the restaurant, her phone rang. It was Drishtant. She became very nervous. She was confused whether to pick up the phone or not. But she knew that if she didn't take the call, then Drishtant would become very suspicious and ask her a hundred questions. So she decided to answer the phone.

"Hi, Drishtant! How are you?"asked Lalsa.

"Where are you? I can hear a lot of noise and music around you," Drishtant asked inquisitively.

"Oh actually, I have come to a restaurant for lunch."

"With your father?"

"Yes, yes," Lalsa answered hurriedly.

"Where is he now?"

"He has gone to the washroom," Lalsa was nervous.

"Okay, call me when you are free," Drishtant disconnected the phone.

Lalsa was literally sweating. She was not in the habit of lying but just to avoid the wrath of Drishtant, she lied. Earlier, she had decided to tell everything to Drishtant but after lying to him, she didn't know what to do.

At night, Lalsa called Sanya.

"You mean girl! How could you do this to me? We were inseparable in school for nine years and we are no less than twin sisters. But suddenly you vanished and completely forgot about me as if I never existed in your life," Sanya said in a hurtful voice.

"Sanya, please forgive me. I absolutely agree with you that I committed a mistake by not sharing my new number with you. Actually my mobile phone fell in the toilet and conked out completely. I didn't have anyone's contact number. You remember, on the last day of school, all of us created and exchanged our email ID's, which I had saved in my mobile, so those details too got lost."

"Okay! But you could have put in more efforts to reach out to me. If I were you, I would have come to Delhi to meet you. But how did you get my number? Did you meet Robin?"

"Yes, he met me today in Delhi."

"Oh wow, Lalsa! You are very lucky to find such a nice boy who waited for you so patiently. He was dying to talk to you. I gave him your email ID last week. He said that he would go to Delhi and give you a surprise. Believe me, he loves you truly and can do anything for your happiness. You must also be very happy to meet him again!"

"Hmmm...But there is a twist in my story," Lalsa said in a low voice.

"What do you mean? Did you find someone else?" Sanya got suspicious.

"Hmm..."

"No, no! You can't do this to him, Lalsa!" Sanya was genuinely concerned for Robin.

"But it was destined to happen, Sanya that's why my mobile phone conked out and I lost connection with Robin. I thought he had dumped me. At that time, Drishtant entered in my life and swept me off my feet completely with his love and care."

"Did you tell this to Robin?"

"Yes Sanya, I told him the truth."

"What did he say? How did he react?"

"Obviously, he was hurt but I think he will be fine, I hope he will understand my situation and not misunderstand me. I guess, we will always be very good friends."

"Okay! Anyway, if you are happy, then I am happy too. In any case, I have to stand by you, not Robin."

Lalsa told her everything about Drishtant but deliberately hid his negative traits. Sanya felt happy to know that Lalsa was happy.

Next day, Drishtant returned to Delhi. She was in college when suddenly Drishtant called her up and asked her to come out. He was sitting in the car. Lalsa opened the door and got in.

"Hi! How are you? You were supposed to come tomorrow, but why did you change your programme?" Lalsa asked smilingly. Drishtant didn't answer but kept driving the car at a high speed.

"What has happened, Drishtant?" Lalsa asked worriedly. Her heart was in her mouth. She could feel that she was going to have a tough time. Drishtant stopped the car at a secluded place in Rajinder Nagar. He then turned towards her and asked with a frown, "So you were with your father yesterday?"

"What do you mean, Drishtant? Why are you asking me this question?" Lalsa asked fearfully.

"Answer me, yes or no."

Lalsa didn't answer. Her silence further exasperated Drishtant. He banged his fist on the dashboard and shouted,

"Tell me the truth! Shikha told me that your father is out of station and you were trying to fool me? Tell me now, were you with your father?" Drishtant started shouting.

Lalsa got frightened. "No!" she mumbled.

"Who was with you?" Drishtant asked in a threatening manner. He held her by her shoulders and sternly looked into her eyes. Lalsa started trembling.

"Calm down, Drishtant! I will tell you everything. I didn't want to hide anything from you."

"You didn't want to hide anything from me, that's why you lied to me. Tell me who that bastard was! Tell me fast!" Drishtant was beyond himself.

"Robin!" Lalsa sputtered.

"Who is Robin?"

"He was my friend when I was studying in Mussoorie."

"You never told me that you had any boyfriend. How many more boyfriends do you have?" Drishtant asked furiously.

"He was just a casual friend," Lalsa mumbled.

"Okay, how many more casual boyfriends do you have with whom you meet outside your house without telling your parents?"

"No, Drishtant, it is not like that. There was nothing between us. You are misunderstanding me. He had come from London and wanted to meet me for a while." Lalsa started crying. But her tears couldn't distract Drishtant's anger.

"Okay, if he was your casual friend, then why did you meet him alone? Don't lie, Lalsa! Admit it that he was your boyfriend. Say that he was your boyfriend!" Drishtant's face and eyes had turned red with rage.

Lalsa got nervous.

"Yes!" she admitted.

"Immediately get out of my car. Get lost and never show me your face again." He opened the door next to her seat and pulled her out. Lalsa burst into tears. This kind of humiliation broke her.

With her legs shaking, she walked for about 20 minutes with trembling legs towards the main road to get a cab. She was in a deplorable condition. She kept her handkerchief on her eyes to hide her tears while sitting in the cab. The cab driver observed her crying and asked, "Madam *ji*! Are you fine?"

"Yes *bhaiya*, I am fine! I am not feeling well, please drive fast."

"Okay, Madam *ji*!" the cab driver changed the gear to increase the speed of the vehicle.

Lalsa's house help opened the door. Thankfully, her mother was not at home. Her servant offered to serve the lunch, but she refused and told him not to disturb her. She rushed to her room, locked the door and fell down on her bed like a log. She kept on crying for hours. Drishtant had misbehaved with her as if she was a criminal. Without even giving her a chance to explain, he had completely dismissed her. She loved him truly and had no intentions of betraying him but he didn't even give her a chance to explain herself.

In the evening, when her mother came back she asked Lalsa to open the door. "What happened, Lalsa? Ram told me that you are not well." Her mother was worried after looking at her face. Lalsa's swollen eyes and red cheeks clearly showed that she had been crying for long.

"Nothing much, Mom. I had a stomach ache. Now, I am fine!" Lalsa said with a fake smile.

"Who are you trying to fool, Lalsa? I know Drishtant must have hurt you again. Why don't you leave him?" her mother said furiously.

Lalsa didn't say anything but helpless tears coursed down her cheeks.

Wiping her tears, her mother said lividly, "Just listen to me. From now on, I will not let you talk to him. If he ever tries to contact you, then I will not spare him."

Lalsa could not stop herself. She hugged her mother and started sobbing loudly. "He doesn't know me well. I am going to teach him a bitter lesson. How dare he hurt you so badly?" Her mother was exasperated.

After crying for a while, Lalsa felt better. She kissed her mother's cheek and said, "Mom, don't worry I am fine now!"

"Give me his number. I want to talk to him right now." her mother insisted.

"No, Mom there is no need to talk to him anymore."

"Lalsa, I have seen you suffering a lot since long in this relationship. Just remember, when any relationship gives you more pain than love, it is better to draw a line and quit. You are not even engaged to him. Don't even think twice and get rid of him," said her mother firmly.

"Yes, you are right, Mom! I will never talk to him," Lalsa said in determined voice.

In the evening, when Shikha came to meet her, she was shocked to see Lalsa's condition. Lalsa didn't hide anything from her and told her everything about Robin and her brief relationship with him. She further told Shikha that she would not continue any relationship with Drishtant in future. Shikha didn't have the courage to convince Lalsa to forgive Drishtant once again. She had never imagined that Drishtant could go to such an extent. With a heavy heart, she left after a while.

19

Bitter Memories

Drishtant was very upset. Lalsa was the first and last girl in his life whom he loved from the depth of his soul. Her truthful and sincere eyes with innocent face reflecting her pristine soul had entranced him at the very first sight. His heart told him that someone like Lalsa would never betray anyone. But he was so wrong. She also betrayed him like his mother, who had betrayed him and his father. Before meeting Lalsa, he was determined to never get involved with any girl. He didn't want to repeat history. He didn't want to be vulnerable to the extent where anyone like his mother could hurt him again. Once again, bitter memories of his past shrouded his mind.

His mother was very beautiful. Her father served in the Indian Foreign Services, so she had travelled the world. She had a strong personality because of which she always stood out in the crowd. She was also exceptionally talented. Once she had painted Drishtant's portrait which was still hanging in his bedroom.

His father, on the other hand, was a workaholic who spent most of his time in his business engagements. A sense of belonging to each other was missing between them. They hardly spent time together. Although they were married to each other but they were not each other's companion. Their relationship was very formal, with minimum conversation and nominal physical proximity. But at that time, Drishtant was too young to understand his parents' relationship.

He lost his mother when he was nine years old. During her lifetime, she did not let Drishtant sleep on the pillow. He always slept on one of her arms. His father had a snoring problem. Therefore, he would sleep in a different bedroom. At times, Drishtant's father would come to their room to call his mother. His mother would switch on the TV and tell him to watch a cartoon film for a while. She would go to his father's bedroom for less than half an hour, and return to hug and sleep with Drishtant. She devoted her whole life to Drishtant. Whether it was preparing his tiffin box, dropping him to school or teaching or playing with him, she was always with him.

He still remembered vividly that she could always read his mind to his surprise. One day, while sitting on his mother's lap, he started staring at her face sadly. His mother immediately asked, "Why do you look so sad, son? Are you wondering, what if I die? Don't worry. I will always be with you," she said with an exuberant laugh.

How wrong was she!

Suddenly, things began to change. One day, his mother took him to a restaurant to meet a man. He was a very good-looking, learned and confident person. He talked to his mother in fluent English. Drishtant still remembered their conversation.

The man held his mother's hand and said, "I am still waiting for you. I have never lost the hope of marrying you. You know, I love you. I could not marry you ten years ago because my career was not settled back then but now I can look after you and your son. Please come back into my life which is like a desolate and parched desert without you. My feelings are still the same. I know you also love me, so without wasting even a day, please come back to me as we have only one life."

The man broke down and his mother's eyes were also moist. She looked at Drishtant, and realising his presence, she withdrew her hand in embarrassment.

"It is not that easy now!" she answered politely.

"I will die without you. Only then will you understand my love," he insisted.

"Don't be foolish! You will always be my best friend but don't expect more than that from me. I respect your feelings but try to understand that I am the mother of a child and a wife to someone else, so nothing of this sort is possible now. Please move on! I have to leave now." She held Drishtant's hand and stood up to leave.

On her way back, she said, "Drishtant, you are very young to understand everything, but I want to tell you that Sambandh and I are childhood friends. We wanted to marry each other but my parents didn't wait for him to get settled. Now he is an IAS officer. I don't want to hide anything about my life from you. That's why I wanted you to be with me while meeting him."

"Will you marry him, Mom?" Drishtant asked a bit scared.

"No, it is not possible now, my boy," she said with a loud hollow laugh. "One more thing, please don't tell anything to your father about him."

Drishtant kept his promise.

After that day, it was never the same. His mother started to indulge in long chats on the phone with Sambandh. At night, she would try to put him to sleep early in order to talk to Sambandh. The scenario changed. Drishtant was not the only person whom she loved. This man had snatched a larger portion of her mother's attention, time and love which once exclusively belonged to him. Earlier, whenever he got up at night, he would find himself clinging to his mother and sleeping on her arm. But now, whenever he got up, he found his mother turned towards the other side, whispering on the phone. He felt very sad but never uttered a word about it. His mother who could always read his feelings without saying anything was now too engrossed in someone else and her love to notice his grief. She had found her companion, who she had been missing throughout her life.

One day, Sambandh was invited for dinner to their place. His mother introduced him to her husband as an old family friend. He cordially shook hands with Drishtant's father. He ruffled Drishtant's hair.

"Hi, handsome!" he said with a smile.

Drishtant didn't answer as he hated him for snatching his mother's love from him. After they finished dinner, his father went to his bedroom to have his medicine. The same second, Sambandh got up and kissed his mother's hand brazenly. His mother was taken aback. Shyly she said, "Behave!"

For the first time in his life, Drishtant hated his mother because she did not slap that person. He could not sleep that night and felt very lonely.

Drishtant's summer vacation was about to commence when one night he heard his mother talk on the phone, "Don't worry! Drishtant's summer vacation will start from next week. I will go to my mom's house. There I will discuss with my mother about your marriage proposal. Trust me, after marriage, you will be happy forever and I will also feel completely relieved."

He understood that his mother was planning to marry Sambandh. He felt a strange fear. He wanted to vomit. He loved his mother but didn't want to leave his father, his cousins and everyone forever. He felt helpless. He wondered how parents could take such ruthless decisions without considering the plight of their children. In order to make their own life complete and perfect, they didn't mind making their children's life incomplete and imperfect.

In the morning, his mother was dropping him to school. On the way, she asked smilingly, "Drishtant, tell me one thing. If you have to choose between your father and me, whom would you choose?" Drishtant felt like a loser who had lost his mother forever to that man.

"Tell me, son!" She asked with a laugh.

"If I don't come with you, will you leave me and go away?" Drishtant questioned back. His mother turned pale. She bit her lips with her teeth and hugged him tight close to her chest.

"Never, my baby!" she said with moist eyes.

But Drishtant knew the truth. His mother's priorities had changed. Drishtant knew that she would go away even if he didn't accompany her.

That night, when his mother tried to hug him in bed, he turned away. He did not feel like hugging her. Next morning, when he was in the school, he was called back home urgently. His uncle had come to take him back.

"Why are you taking me back so early?" Drishtant asked. Tears rolled down from his uncle's eyes. He hugged him tightly and said, "Your mother met with an accident while she was on her way to the bank. She is in the hospital and wants to see you."

Drishtant was stunned to find everyone crying near the emergency ward. He was immediately taken to the emergency ward by his father. He saw his mother in a semi -conscious state, repeatedly calling out his name. She had severe injuries and her head was covered in bandage.

"Open your eyes. Look, Drishtant has come," his father said as his voice choked. His mother opened her eyes and tried to raise her hand to touch Drishtant. His father kept his hand in her mother's hand. She tried hard to fix her gaze on his face, with her unfocused eyes and pressed his hand as hard as she could. Tears rolled down her cheeks.

"Sorry, son! I have to go!" she said, then gasped for her last breath and left forever.

After his mother's death, Drishtant was completely shattered and lonely. She meant everything to him. It became very difficult for him to trust anyone or share his vulnerabilities. But Lalsa's arrival in his life changed his perspective. Gradually, he felt he could open up and fell in love with her. But in his heart, he always felt insecure. He didn't want anyone to snatch her away from him like his mother. That's why he wanted to protect her from everyone's eyes. He felt that Lalsa was very innocent and it was important to keep an eye on her, so that she didn't go astray. He never knew that she already had someone in her life like his mother. She had never ever mentioned that boy and this insincerity had broken his heart. He decided to break up with her forever. Even after several efforts made by Shikha to convince him that Lalsa had a very brief relationship with Robin and that too before she had met him, Drishtant was not convinced. Finally, Vrinda decided to talk to him.

"Drishtant, why aren't you talking to Lalsa?"

"She is a cheat like my mother." Drishtant said bitterly.

"Who told you this? Your mother was not a cheat!" Vrinda was astonished to hear his view for his mother.

"No, you don't know the reality."

"I know everything, Drishtant! We were like sisters, she confided completely in me."

"No, you don't know Vindy Aunty. She cheated my father. She had decided to get married to her old friend Sambandh."

"No son, you are wrong! Sambandh loved your mother but for her, he was only a good friend."

"But she had made all the plans to go to her parents' house and marry him. I overheard this with my own ears."

"No, she wasn't planning to marry him. Instead she had convinced Sambandh to marry her maternal cousin. In fact, Sambandh had liked the girl and your mother was planning to go to Mumbai to finalise everything with her mother. But unfortunately, she died before that. Later on, Sambandh married the same girl which your mother had chosen for him. "But they talked every night," said Drishtant.

So what? They were childhood friends, and shared their thoughts and emotions. They had so many fond memories to recall and so many new things to discuss. That's why they enjoyed talking to each other. Was that a crime? Didn't she have a right to be happy? She also needed a friend to talk to and share things with. She never found a companion in your father. Your parents were inherently incompatible and that was the reason for their loneliness. They didn't have any connect, neither physical, nor emotional. It was a completely dead relationship which was not worth continuing for even a single day. But still she decided to continue her relationship with your father just because of you. It is a man's world. Even you blamed her for everything very conveniently but never tried to find out the reality."

Drishtant had no answer. He realised that he had been too self-centred and selfish while judging his mother. He had been very bitter towards her and felt guilty for hating his mother for so many years.

He was too shattered and confused about the future of his relationship with Lalsa. He didn't know whether Lalsa had betrayed him or his own madness and possessiveness had snatched her away from him. He knew that Lalsa would never forgive him for his terrible behaviour. He decided not to contact Lalsa until he had changed himself.

20

Mother Gets Suspicious

Lalsa stopped talking to Drishtant. Even he didn't try to contact her. Lalsa wanted to forget her relationship with Drishtant completely. She wanted to cut the portion which belonged to Drishtant completely out of her life. There were times Lalsa wondered why she was so unlucky in love? She had come close to two boys in her life and it did not work out with either of them. Robin was placid, shy, and respectful, while Drishtant was a smug, possessive and an aggressive lover who treated her like a commodity and tried to possess her. She left Robin because of Drishtant, who left her because of his possessiveness. She promised herself not to mingle again with any boy and decided to pay attention to her parents and studies.

Shikha was still her best friend. Although, her mother wanted to ban her entry in the house but Lalsa convinced her that Shikha was innocent and wasn't aware of anything. After a few days, Shikha told her that Drishtant had left for London to pursue his Masters in Business Management.

Lalsa again started spending most of her time with Shikha. They had become inseparable companions to each other once again. She helped her to fill the void left by Drishtant in her life.

Three months passed by, and Lalsa tried her best to curb the agony of separation from Drishtant. Neither she nor Shikha ever discussed him as Shikha knew that Drishtant had inflicted tremendous damage on Lalsa. In her heart, Shikha felt guilty for pursuing Lalsa to be in a relationship with Drishtant. She had never expected him to behave in such a ghastly manner with Lalsa. Not even in her wildest dream had she expected such atrocious behaviour from him. She was trying her best to compensate and make Lalsa happy.

One night before sleeping, Lalsa got a call on her mobile. It was an overseas call. She picked up the phone.

"Hello," said Lalsa. There was no answer from the other side. She again said, "Hello."

Finally, somebody mumbled, "Love you! Love you! Love you!" and disconnected the phone. Lalsa was shocked. She wondered who could it possibly be–Robin, Drishtant or some psycho? Robin was too sober and Drishtant was too angry to call her. She convinced herself that maybe it was a wrong number. She decided to forget about the phone call and sleep but missed Drishtant terribly. She heaved a deep sigh and decided to go to her mother's room to change her mood. When Lalsa entered her mother's room, she saw her mother crying.

"What happened, Mom? Are you alright? Are you missing Dad?" Lalsa asked.

"Nothing much. You go and leave me alone for some time," said her mother.

"Why are you talking like this? What are you hiding from me? Tell me the truth please."

Her mother started crying loudly.

"What happened, Mom? For God's sake, don't scare me and tell me the truth."

"You know Mrs Puri, my friend who meets us in Roshnara Club quite often?"

"Yes, yes! What happened to her?"

"She called me and said that today she saw your father in a movie hall with a lady."

"What? Where did she see him? But he has been in Bikaner for the last two days."

"Yes, I told her the same thing but she was very sure."

"*Uffo*! You know Mom, it is not possible. How could you believe someone without any proof and doubt Dad without any rhyme or reason?" Lalsa said irritably.

"This is not the first time, Lalsa. This has happened earlier too. Two months back, one of my friends saw him with a lady in the mall."

"This is not possible, Mom! Dad will come back tomorrow morning. We will talk to him. Now please calm down and have dinner with me since I am feeling very hungry."

Lalsa wiped the tears from her mother's cheeks. She was absolutely confident about her father's fidelity. He was an exceptionally loving man who would never ditch his wife and daughter. Lalsa dragged her mother to the dining hall and had dinner with her.

"Should I sleep with you tonight?"

"No, no! I am fine now."

"Okay, Mom! Good night!" Lalsa went to her bedroom to sleep.

21

Lalsa Visits Mumbai

Summer vacation had started and Shikha went to London for two months with her family. They had a flat in London where Drishtant had already been staying. Shikha told Lalsa on the phone that a Pakistani girl was in love with Drishtant but he was not interested. She also told Lalsa that he had been visiting a counsellor regularly to sort out his emotional problems which he didn't share with her.

Lalsa was upset and jealous too. She never knew that she was still so possessive about Drishtant. The thought of his proximity with another girl bothered her. Her attachment with Drishtant was still stronger than her annoyance for him.

Her mother could feel Lalsa's agony but didn't know how to pacify her. She suggested Lalsa go to Mumbai to her uncle's house and spend a few days there. Lalsa's *mamu* (maternal uncle) was working in a multinational company. He had been posted in Mumbai for the last five years. He had two daughters–Neha and Nidhi. Neha was eight years older than Nidhi. Two years ago, she married a NRI and settled in London. Nidhi and Lalsa were of the same age and were very close to each other. She was the one with whom Lalsa could share all the secrets of her life without any inhibitions.

Lalsa agreed to go to Mumbai as she also wanted some respite from the bitter memories of Drishtant.

Lalsa reached Mumbai. Nidhi came to pick her up from the airport. She was very excited to have Lalsa in Mumbai. They hugged each other and Nidhi warmly kissed her on her cheek. They held each other's hand tight and walked to their car.

"Hey Lalsa, you can't imagine how much fun we are going to have together. Remember, I will not let you go before a month as I have already prepared a long list of programmes for you. One more thing, Neha *didi* is also coming tomorrow after two years along with *jeeju*. You know what? She is pregnant and wants to give birth to her first child in Mumbai. It is a tradition in our Punjabi families that girls give birth to their first child at the mother's parents' home. I think, the possible logic behind it could be that the girl feels more comfortable with her parents, isn't it?"

Nidhi at last stopped and looked at Lalsa for affirmation. Lalsa smiled at her excitement and affection. She had always been very lively and talkative. Nidhi noticed that nothing excited Lalsa who was otherwise a chirpy girl and as lively as she was. She nudged Lalsa with her elbow after sitting in the car and asked, "What happened, Lalsa? What is wrong with you? You look sad. Is everything fine?"

"Yes!" Lalsa said with a fake smile. Nidhi slapped her gently on her cheek and said, "You know you can't hide anything from me, so tell me the truth."

Lalsa laughed at her persistence. She knew that Nidhi was right. She would not be able to hide anything from her for long. She started her story. There was a traffic jam and meanwhile Lalsa shared everything about her relationship with Drishtant.

Nidhi listened to her with patience and concentration. She fumed with anger every now and then but continued to listen to Lalsa. In the end, she burst out angrily, "My God, Lalsa! How could you take so much of nonsense from anybody? I have always known you to have self-esteem and confidence. But you compromised your values by bearing with his toxic behaviour unnecessarily. What has happened to you? Why did you become so weak and vulnerable? What was so special about him for which you continued your relationship with him?" Nidhi asked.

Tears rolled down Lalsa's cheeks. She wiped her tears and said, "His immense love, care and sincerity."

"What rubbish, Lalsa! I would never buy all these attributes at the cost of my self-respect. Anyway, forget about that loser. It is his loss. You are the best girl and deserve the best. Believe me, in future, you will find someone much better than Drishtant. While you are here, let's have fun and let go off all the sadness. Who knows, what's going to happen, so let's just live in the moment."

Lalsa felt much better after she shared her sorrow with Nidhi who gave her a patient hearing without judging her. Then they began to plan the day and decided to visit Sidhi Vinayak Temple after which they agreed mutually to take a stroll down Juhu Beach.

22

Obnoxious Relative

Next day, there was a lot of hustle bustle in the house as Neha was expected to arrive in the evening. The house was done up in order to welcome Neha and her husband. It was a three-bedroom flat in Central Mumbai. Neha's mother had prepared the choicest of dishes, since Neha was visiting them after a long time. It was late in the evening when Neha arrived and the house was full of noise, joy and warmth.

Neha looked more beautiful with the glow on her face that reflected the happiness of an expectant mother. Lalsa had never met Neha's husband, Rohan. He seemed to be in his early thirties. Rohan had a charming aura. Neha hugged Lalsa affectionately with a bright smile and said, "Good to see you Lalsa after so long. You look so pretty."

"Come, Rohan meet my little sister, Lalsa!" Neha said enthusiastically.

Rohan shook hands with Lalsa. While he shook hands with her, he slyly rubbed his thumb on her palm in circular motion in a peculiar manner. Lalsa looked at his face shockingly and found a flirtatious smile and ravenous look on his face. She didn't know how to react. Immediately, she tried to pull her hand back. But Rohan resisted and released her hand sluggishly. Everyone was busy chatting and eating till late in the night but Rohan's eyes were fixed on Lalsa's face, which made her very uncomfortable.

At night, while sleeping with Nidhi, Lalsa wanted to share the reason of her discomfort with her but decided to keep quiet and ignore Rohan's advances for the moment.

Next day, after having breakfast, Nidhi and her mother went to attend a prayer meeting for someone who had passed away in their neighbourhood and *mamu* went to his office. Neha and her husband went to their bedroom to rest. Lalsa also went to her bedroom and slouched on the sofa to watch television. Suddenly, there was a knock on the door. She got up immediately to open the door anticipating Neha's return. But to her dismay, it was Rohan.

"Hi!" he said with an evil smile.

Lalsa composed herself. She immediately blocked one side of the door with her body and another with her arm. Her bedroom door opened into the drawing room.

"Oh, *jeeja ji*! Let's sit there!" she pointed to the sofa in the drawing room.

"Why can't we sit in your room?" Rohan said, looking deep into her eyes.

Lalsa changed her gaze without budging an inch and said, "Actually my room is totally messed up. We can sit in the drawing room comfortably. We will call *didi* also." Without waiting further, she screamed loudly, "Neha *didi*!"

Rohan put his hand on her lips and murmured, "Hey! What are you doing? Don't call her! She is sleeping. I have some secret to share with you. Come, let us sit in the drawing room." Rohan could sense that the gentle Lalsa had suddenly become determined and angry. There was no trace of fear on her face.

"Actually, tomorrow is Neha's birthday. I wanted to get a surprise gift for her but I am not acquainted with the local market, so I wanted to request you to please accompany me to buy a gift for her."

"But I am also new to Mumbai. I will not be able to guide you much about the markets."

"The driver can take us to the market but at least help me to choose a gift as it is the first chance for me to buy a gift for her on my own. Please help me! Please!" pleaded Rohan. Lalsa was not comfortable in his company but decided to accompany him instead of creating a scene.

Lalsa's uncle had hired a chauffeur-driven Mercedes for Rohan. The driver took them to Zaveri jewellers. They bought two diamond necklaces. Rohan wanted to have lunch with Lalsa but she insisted on going back and having lunch at home. On the way back, the chauffeur was driving the car and both of them were sitting quietly in the back seat.

Suddenly, Rohan placed his hand on her hand, and started singing, "*Wo saadgi kahen ise, deewangi kahen, unka badha jo haath, yahan dil luta diya.*" Lalsa pulled back her hand forcefully with a stern look.

"Aren't you scared of *didi*? Please don't force me to tell her everything," Lalsa said in a determined voice.

"Scared of *didi*?" Rohan chortled mockingly. She is enjoying the life of a queen because of me. She is nothing without me. Do you think she can even raise her voice in front of me?"

Lalsa felt like slapping him but stopped herself. Meanwhile, they reached the house. Lalsa opened the door immediately and hurriedly headed towards the lift without waiting for Rohan. Neha was sitting in the drawing room.

"Where were you, Lalsa? I was looking for you. Even Rohan is not in the house. Have you seen him?" She asked worriedly. Before Lalsa could say anything, she heard Rohan's voice behind her back.

"Actually, Neha we were bored, so both of us went for a drive. Anyway, how are you feeling, my darling?" He said lovingly and pecked her cheek and hugged her. Neha was apparently not amused after knowing that Rohan was with Lalsa. But her disturbed and suspicious eyes suddenly turned soft and seemed reassured after Rohan's cuddling. Lalsa was feeling exasperated. But she didn't want to hurt Neha during her pregnancy.

"Excuse me!" Lalsa said and rushed to her room.

After half an hour, Nidhi and her mother were back. Lunch had been laid. Lalsa was feeling very exhausted emotionally and didn't feel like seeing Rohan's face again. Suddenly, she felt very lonely and unsafe. She excused herself, saying that she had a headache so she would eat later.

In the evening, everyone decided to dine out. Lalsa was least interested but could not find any excuse to duck out of the programme. She was very careful not to look at Rohan. They went to Taj hotel and had Chinese food. Lalsa's uncle wanted to pay the bill but Rohan had already given his card to the waiter. Everyone felt grateful because of Rohan's generosity. But Lalsa knew that he was trying to show off by flaunting his money. Nidhi was concerned because of Lalsa's unusual silence. But Lalsa convinced her by saying that she was feeling a little low because of a headache.

Once back, everyone decided to sit in the drawing room and chat. At midnight, a cake was cut by Neha and everyone congratulated her. Rohan gifted her one of the necklaces which was highly appreciated by everyone. Lalsa wondered why he didn't he gift her both the necklaces. Maybe he wanted to surprise Neha the next day with the second necklace. Therefore, she decided to keep quiet. Moreover, she didn't want to interfere unnecessarily in Rohan's affairs.

Next day, a small party was held to celebrate Neha's birthday. About 20 guests were expected. The furniture of the drawing room was rearranged. The dining chairs were adjusted in the sitting area to create more space. Everyone was getting ready. Lalsa came out of the room as Nidhi wanted to change her clothes. She was sitting in the drawing room when suddenly Rohan saw her and rushed towards her. Hurriedly, he took out an envelope from his pocket and dropped it in her lap.

"This is for you, my dear!" He said with a wink and a flying kiss and disappeared in a jiffy. Lalsa was taken aback. She quickly opened the envelope and found the second diamond necklace they had bought for Neha in the envelope. She didn't know what to do with the necklace. Meanwhile, she saw Rohan and Neha coming out of their room together. By then Lalsa knew what to do. She immediately said in a loud voice.

"See *jeeju,* you are so forgetful! You left your envelope here," Lalsa said with a victorious smile. Rohan's face turned pale. He had not expected such a smart and spontaneous move from Lalsa.

"Yes! Yes!" He murmured and took the envelope from Lalsa immediately, turned towards Neha and said brazenly, "One more surprise gift for my love." Neha opened the envelope and hugged her husband in excitement.

"Thank you so much, Rohan! You have made my day! You are the best husband in this world!"

Lalsa genuinely hated Rohan for his audacity. She wondered how anyone could be so shameless. But she decided to keep silent as she was a guest in their house for a few days. So she decided not to disturb the peace of their happy family.

Throughout the party, she kept herself away from Rohan's reach and gaze. Thankfully next morning, Rohan had to leave for Germany to participate in an exhibition for ten days from where he would proceed to London. He was expected to come back at the time of the birth of his child. Lalsa promised herself not to meet Rohan ever in her life.

The next five days were very entertaining for Lalsa. Nidhi took her to night clubs, lunches and movies. She made special arrangements for Lalsa through her acquaintance to watch a film shoot of Lalsa's favourite actor, Ranbir Kapoor. Lalsa was thrilled to shake hands and get a warm hug from him. After Rohan's departure, she was treated as the guest of honour of the house. Even Neha became very warm towards her.

23

The Horror is Back

Lalsa's happy days ended very soon. One morning, when all of them were having breakfast, the doorbell rang. The house help opened the door. To Lalsa's horror, it was Rohan standing in the doorway with the same brazen smile.

"Surprise! I am back! Hi everyone!" he waved his hand in the air. Everyone was surprised, rather shocked by his sudden arrival. Even Neha could not hide her feelings.

"It seems no one is happy to see me again," he said with a fake smile.

"No! No! Welcome, welcome!" Lalsa's uncle said and immediately rushed to take his bag from his hand.

"Actually, I missed Neha so much that I couldn't stop myself from coming back." Rohan lied.

Everyone stood up to welcome him. Rohan touched Lalsa's aunt and uncle's feet and hugged Nidhi and Neha. Lalsa deliberately stood behind all of them to escape from his touch. When Rohan looked at her, she waved her hand and said, "Hi, *jeeju*!"

"Why are you standing so far?" Rohan reached out to her, hugged her and moved his hand on her back in a slimy manner. Lalsa shuddered.

"Come join us for breakfast!" Lalsa's aunt invited Rohan.

"Sure! Sure!" Rohan said and sat on the vacant chair of the dining table. It had become difficult for Lalsa to swallow even a single bite after his arrival.

"How are you girls? Hope you are having a nice time here, Lalsa!" Rohan asked. Lalsa didn't say anything. She nodded in affirmation without looking at him.

Next morning, her uncle was having a bath, and her aunt was in the kitchen preparing breakfast for everyone. Neha went to the washroom to freshen up. Lalsa came out of the room in search of the newspaper. She saw Rohan reading the newspaper in the drawing room.

"Good morning, Lalsa! I think you want the newspaper. You can have it as I am done with it." He stood up and while handing over the newspaper to Lalsa, he caught hold of her hand.

"Lalsa, why are you doing this to me? You must be thinking I am paranoid. Yes, you are right! I am genuinely getting mad. Believe me, I can't live without you. This is the reason I cut my Germany visit short and came back within five days. Just because of you. I have never ever missed any girl like this before and I want you in my life, Lalsa. We should get married. I will keep you very happy. Please! Please marry me!" Rohan pleaded. Lalsa pulled her hand away forcefully and ran to her bedroom without answering. She was gasping for breath when Nidhi came out of the toilet.

"What happened, Lalsa? Are you okay?"asked Nidhi worriedly. Lalsa was sitting on the bed and Nidhi was standing near Lalsa trying to pacify her. Lalsa held her tight and started crying.

"Oh my god, what happened Lalsa? Is everything fine? Should I call Papa?"

"No!" Lalsa said.

"Okay, let me shut the door and then tell me everything clearly." Nidhi locked the door. Lalsa shared every bit with Nidhi who was stunned to hear the whole story.

"What should we do now? Should we tell everything to Neha *didi* and everyone else?" Nidhi seemed confused.

"No, I don't want to ruin *didi's* married life. Please book my ticket. I want to go back to Delhi."

"Lalsa, you can't go like this. *Jeeju* has come for only three days. We can plan to go to Shirdi tomorrow and come back the day after, late in the evening. By then *jeeju* would have left. Please bear him for today. Then you don't have to see his face ever again. Is that okay with you?" Nidhi asked, while holding Lalsa's face by her chin.

"Okay!" said Lalsa and smiled with tearful eyes.

"You have a bath. I will get our breakfast in the room."

Both of them had their breakfast in the bedroom. After that, Nidhi took Lalsa to her friend's house. They came back in the evening. Lalsa's aunt had gone to the market and her uncle had not yet come back from his office. Rohan was sitting in the drawing room as if he was waiting for them.

"I was looking for you! Where did both of you disappear?" Rohan sounded irritated.

"Why, *jeeju*? Why were you looking for us? You came here for *didi*. You must spend your time with her. Why did you need us?" Nidhi asked stingingly.

"Not me, Nidhi but Neha wanted to see you. She is waiting for you in her room," said Rohan. Nidhi went to see Neha while Lalsa rushed to her room without giving him a chance to talk. But Rohan followed her hurriedly to the room, hugged her amorously and tried to kiss her lips. Lalsa got violent. She slapped him hard on his face and shouted loudly, "Nidhi! Nidhi!"

Nidhi and Neha came running towards her room. Nidhi hugged Lalsa who had started crying.

"What happened, Lalsa?" asked Neha with a pale face.

"*Didi*, this monster tried to kiss me," Lalsa answered sobbingly.

"She is lying!" Rohan said in a loud voice.

"No *didi*, I am not lying!" pleaded Lalsa.

"Lalsa, I think you are mistaken. He is not like that. He is a very sober person." Neha said lovingly while patting on her head.

"No *didi*!" Nidhi intervened to disclose the truth about Rohan.

But Neha stopped her by raising her hand and said sternly, "Enough! Lalsa, get some rest. Nidhi you look after her. Rohan let's go to our room." She said and left the room with Rohan. Nidhi was livid because of the whole episode. She wanted to show Rohan's real face to her sister but Neha was not ready to listen to anyone. When Nidhi's mother returned, she narrated the whole episode to her. Her mother, with folded hands requested Lalsa to not tell the reality to her uncle and her parents.

At night, Rohan and Neha went out for dinner. Nidhi had to attend her friend's birthday. She was reluctant to go but Lalsa forced her to go for a while. Nidhi requested her to join her but Lalsa declined as she was too upset to go anywhere.

Lalsa was very upset. Inspite of her aunt's insistence she hardly ate anything. She was too sad to sleep as she missed Drishtant and cried till late in the night.

He was so protective towards her and really cared for her. Even though he fought with her but he was always there for her. He had gifted her a gold chain with a locket of Lord Shiva. After their separation, she had never worn that chain but had always carried it in her bag. She had taken off the chain but hadn't dare to throw it out of her life. That night, once again she took out, kissed the chain and wore it around her neck. She felt a strange sense of peace and security.

She remembered her first kiss with him. She anticipated that they would kiss but she was taken aback when one night, while they were coming back from a party, Drishtant stopped the car at a secluded road and kissed her. His lips were warm and a little hard. He kissed her with fervour. It happened so unexpectedly that she was left stunned. She didn't sleep that night and kept revisiting those beautiful moments. He was the person whom she had loved the most. She liked Robin but the depth of love which she had for Drishtant was incomparable.

Tears rolled down from her eyes. Nobody had loved her as Drishtant did. Had he controlled his anger and possessiveness, she would never have dreamt of going away from him.

She also remembered Sanya as she was the closest friend with whom she had shared every secret of her life. After Sanya had moved to London, Lalsa felt her voice of reason had gone missing. She decided to talk to her. Sanya was very upset to know about her separation with Drishtant. She remembered how Lalsa was on seventh heaven when she first heard about Drishtant. She never imagined that Lalsa and Drishtant would break up with each other. She knew Lalsa very well and could feel the depth of her agony because of her breakup with Drishtant.

Rohan's behaviour was also very disturbing for Sanya. She wished to be with Lalsa at such a difficult time of her life. They decided to talk more frequently and be in constant touch with each other.

Lalsa was trying to sleep when once again she received an overseas call. She thought that somebody would have dialed a wrong number. Therefore, she ignored the call. However, again she got a call from the same number. Finally, she picked up the phone and heard a whisper from the other side, "I love you! I love you! I love you!" after which the call was disconnected.

24

Reality of Life

Nidhi planned a visit to Shirdi for two days with Lalsa and her friends to avoid Rohan who was scheduled to leave before their return. Early morning, Nidhi and Lalsa left by car for Shirdi Sai Mandir along with Nidhi's two friends. Both her friends were very lively. Lalsa enjoyed a lot in their company. For a brief period of time, Lalsa felt that all her problems had disappeared.

Next day, they started in the afternoon and reached Mumbai late at night. By then, Rohan had left for London. Neha and her father had gone to drop him at the airport. Lalsa and Nidhi were very tired. They had their dinner without waiting for anyone else and retired to their rooms. They had settled down in their beds after having bath when Neha entered the room.

"Hi, girls! How are you? Hope you had a nice time!"

"Yes *didi*!"answered Nidhi. Lalsa didn't say anything as she had not forgiven her for supporting her husband in his wrongdoings. At least she could have heard her privately before reaching any conclusion.

"Did you pray for me?"

"Of course, *didi*!" answered Nidhi quickly.

"But Lalsa didn't pray for me as she is still annoyed with me. Is that right, Lalsa?"

Lalsa didn't answer. Her face turned red with anger remembering the episode.

"Okay! I want to talk to both of you but for God's sake never share our conversation with any one else." she continued.

"First of all, I want to apologise to you, Lalsa! I didn't stand by you that day, in spite of knowing that Rohan was wrong."

Both of them were stunned.

"Did you know the reality, *didi*?"asked Nidhi.

"Yes, I knew it. The day he went with Lalsa for shopping, I sensed that he was trying to lure her. I could anticipate that the second necklace which Lalsa returned to him was gifted to her by Rohan but I never knew that he would stoop to this level."

"How did you know *didi*?" Nidhi asked curiously.

"Because these are his old tactics–luring women with expensive gifts."

"Does it mean that he habitually flirts with other women?" Nidhi asked with anger and disappointment.

"Unfortunately, yes!" Neha answered with a snort.

"But how could you take his infidelity so lightly? Didn't you ever react or try to change him?" Nidhi asked.

"No, I have never taken his infidelity lightly. He has said that he desperately wants to overcome his infidelity. He has repeatedly asked me to give him some time to change. It is very difficult for me but I am trying to help him change for the better. That doesn't mean that I turn a blind eye to his wrongdoings. Misbehaving with my sister or with another woman is simply unpardonable. I have decided to give him one last chance and if he doesn't change soon, then I will divorce him and live my own life with my child."

"But if you were annoyed with him, then why did you take his side that day?" Lalsa asked.

"I didn't say anything to him in front of you and took him to my room because I knew that he would have never accepted his fault publicly and would have created a scene to prove himself right. I chose to ignore it in front of you and make him accept his fault in private. Once we were alone, I confronted him. I threatened him that in future if he misbehaves with any girl, I would leave him immediately and never let him meet his child. He got very scared as he is impatiently waiting to see his baby. He promised me and swore on his unborn child never to repeat such mistakes."

"Doesn't it hurt your conscience and self-respect?" Nidhi asked, feeling hurt herself.

"It does hurt! But Nidhi no one gets a tailor-made partner. In every marriage, both partners have to compromise, then why not compromise with Rohan for some time and try to change him. I am better than some of my other friends who send their husbands willingly to have paid sex. At least, he does not do anything objectionable in front of me."

"But why?" Lalsa was completely confused.

"Economic dependence, fear of leading a lonely and deprived life, concern about children's future and our society are some of the reasons for it. These women say that their husbands meet all their demands, pamper them and take care of their children, therefore, they are ready to adjust. They think that it is not easy to find a good husband in the second marriage, so they let their husbands be in lieu of secure and comfortable life. You will understand all such things after getting married," Neha said with a sad smile.

"But that is not right, *didi*! How could those women compromise with their dignity and self-respect! Instead of making such indecent compromises in marriage, I would prefer to be single," Lalsa answered firmly.

"Yes, you are right, Lalsa!" Nidhi supported her whole heartedly.

"Both of you are very young and full of enthusiasm. I wish destiny never takes you to the stage where you have to compromise in your respective marriages," Neha said and then continued, "Anyway, now both of you keep your promise and don't tell anything to anyone. Not even to your mom, Lalsa!"

"Okay, *didi*!" Lalsa promised.

Neha hugged and kissed both of them, said good night before leaving the room.

Nidhi and Lalsa could not sleep for hours. They kept discussing Neha's logic which did not appeal to them at all. Resolving to never put up with disloyalty or any type of atrocity of their husband in future, Nidhi slept at 2 in the morning but Lalsa could not sleep. She also made a promise to herself to focus on her career and become financially independent. She wondered how Neha could share her husband with anyone else. She had discontinued her relationship with Drishtant because of his possessiveness. All their fights were only for that reason. She began to contemplate whether she had taken the right step to break her relationship with Drishtant. Her eyes got wet with the memory of Drishtant. It was very difficult to forget a person whom you have loved the most in your life. In the morning, Lalsa and Nidhi woke up late. During breakfast, Neha also joined them.

"*Didi*, tell me one thing. I have a friend who loves a person who in turn loves her a lot but misbehaves because of his possessiveness. What should she do?" Lalsa raised the query with which she was preoccupied. Nidhi smiled as she knew that she was talking about herself.

"If he misbehaves only because of his possessiveness, then definitely he gets hurt because of certain things done by your friend which he disapproves. Therefore, your friend should also introspect her actions," Neha answered while putting a spoonful of porridge in her mouth.

"But he always gets annoyed with her because of wrong reasons. For instance, if she wears a short dress, then he would misbehave with her, which is not right. I think she should have all the freedom to wear dresses of her own choice." Lalsa defended herself while placing the fork on the plate angrily.

Neha also stopped eating her porridge and answered calmly, "Whatever is right according to your friend's perspective may be wrong according to her boyfriend's perspective. No one can decide who is right and who is wrong. The most important thing is to know whether the boy is truly in love with her or not. If it is only an infatuation, then it's best to break off without a thought. It is also pertinent to know that how intense is your friend's love for him? Whether her love for him is more important than her choice and ego because ego can come in the way of adjustments while love can happily make adjustments.

"But why only she? He could also adjust according to her wishes," Lalsa argued.

"Yes, of course! If the love is intense, then both partners should try to save the relationship by finding a peaceful solution to avoid perpetual confrontation with each other because true love is far more precious than any other thing."

Lalsa picked up her fork and started knocking the plate instead of eating the omelette while contemplating Neha's logic.

25

Gym Diaries

Lalsa was back from Mumbai. She didn't tell anything to her mother about Rohan as she knew that her mother was very possessive about her and would take a tough stand on the issue.

One month of summer vacation had gone by and Shikha was still in London. Lalsa had gained weight in the span of two months without any additional diet. Kanta advised her to get her blood tests done. The test reports indicated thyroid. The doctor advised her to join a gym to increase her metabolism. Lalsa decided to join the gym.

The gym appeared to be a good place. It was equipped with all kinds of latest equipments. After she filled the form, she was taken to the doctor who was the owner of the gym.

When Lalsa met the doctor, she found him to be a very stylish and chivalrous man. Looking at her papers, he smilingly said, "So you are Lalsa! I have never heard this name before! What does it mean?"

"It means desire," Lalsa smiled too.

"Okay, Lalsa! I will prepare a special diet plan for you and your coach will guide you about your workout. I hope you will join the gym today."

"Yes, doctor!"

"Good! Welcome to our gym, I hope you have a happy workout session," he said and extended his hand towards Lalsa. She had never touched such a warm padded and soft male hand before.

On the very first day of the gym, she was surprised to find Dimpy walking on a treadmill. She was wearing a black top without sleeves, combined with black shorts. She had lost weight and looked really nice.

"Wow Lalsa, it is lovely to see you here. Where have you been? Let's go to the café and have protein shake before you start your workout. Let's celebrate our reunion!"

"Why did you join the gym? You have a perfect body!" Lalsa asked while they were in the queue to place their order.

"I enjoy working out and secondly, I don't want to put on weight. Anyway, what's new? Do you have a boyfriend?"

"No!"

"My God! Such a pretty girl is without a boyfriend?" Dimpy teased her. "I can't imagine my life without my boyfriend Kunal. Did you meet the doctor of the gym? He is so hot! Why don't you try your luck?" Dimpy winked at her.

"Sorry, not interested!" Lalsa said with a smile.

"Life without a boyfriend must be so boring. You know, I meet Kunal everyday at my house."

"How do you manage to call him everyday to your house?" Lalsa was curious.

"My parents go to Roshnara Club everyday after having lunch to play cards and come back late at night. Till then there is no one to intrude into my privacy. Kunal comes to see me every evening and stays with me till late evening. We have a lot of fun everyday."

"Don't you feel scared?" Lalsa was surprised by her guts.

"No, not at all!" Dimpy said with confidence.

They chatted for half an hour and then said goodbye to each other with the promise to meet the next day at the same time.

Next day, Dimpy came late. Lalsa was running on the treadmill when she came near her and whispered, "Lalsa, I have some gossip to share with you, so get rid of your coach and come to the café fast."

"Okay!" Lalsa seemed curious. After ten minutes, Lalsa joined Dimpy who was having protein shake at that time.

"What happened?" Lalsa asked eagerly.

"My God! Lalsa we committed a blunder!"

"Don't create such a suspense! Just tell me quickly!" Lalsa said, while wiping sweat off her face. She tucked the hand towel into her back pocket.

Dimpy started her story, "You know Kunal comes to my house every day. Last night we had a lot of wine and after having fun, we conked out. I woke up at 8 in the morning with a knock on my door. Kunal was not up till then."

"Then, then what happened?" Lalsa stuttered with excitement.

"It was my mother knocking on the door but I didn't open the door and said that I was rushing to take bath as I had to leave immediately for college. I didn't know what to do. He was sleeping on my bed with only half his clothes on his body."

"Then?"

"Then I woke him up and told him to immediately get ready."

"How did he manage to go out?"

"Actually, we live in a doublet. My parents' bedroom, the drawing room and the kitchen are downstairs and my room is upstairs. After knocking on my door, my mother left and went straight to her room downstairs. I watched her movement from the chink of my door. When I found that everything was under control downstairs, I managed to push Kunal out of my house. But just imagine those fifteen minutes of extreme excitement when he was in my bedroom and my parents were downstairs. My heart was fluttering and I was so nervous."

With raised shoulders, eyes wide open and folded hands, Lalsa wondered how that was possible. Both of them burst out laughing.

"You are impossible, Dimpy! Now let me complete my workout," Lalsa said and stood up. Both of them proceeded towards their coaches. But whenever their eyes met, they couldn't stop laughing.

26

Life Turns Topsy Turvy

When Lalsa came back from her college, her father had already reached home. As always, he had brought lots of gifts for Lalsa and a beautiful sari for her mother to wear on Karva Chauth the next day. She was delighted to see her gifts. Lalsa's father came to her bedroom early in the morning at 5.

"What happened, Dad? Why are you bothering me at this hour?"

"Don't you remember today is Karva Chauth and your mother is fasting for my long life. For the last seven years, you were in a hostel. That's why you don't know much about this festival. Your mother will not eat or drink anything after sunrise and before moonrise. But before sunrise, she can eat whatever she wants to, so she is going to have food right now and to respect her sentiments, we will also join her. Let's see what she has cooked today!"

"But I am not hungry, Dad!"

"Come on you lazy girl, your mother is waiting for you downstairs," Vijay dragged her by her arm.

"Okay!" Lalsa surrendered unwillingly and went downstairs to give company to her mother.

In the evening, her father came early to spend more time with them. The moon was expected to rise in the night sky at 8:30 p.m. Every year on Karva Chauth, Lalsa's mother would witness the moon first, touch her husband's feet and then break her fast by drinking water.

At 7:30 p.m., Lalsa's father told them that he had to meet somebody urgently regarding his business and would be back in an hour. He added that if he got late by any chance then Kanta should see the moon and break her fast. But Kanta refused to break her fast in his absence. She kept waiting till 9:00 p.m. and then called Vijay who told her that he would reach in fifteen minutes. She heard a woman's voice in the background. She got very upset and started crying. Lalsa felt very bad for her mother. She called her father but he didn't pick up the phone. After half an hour, he was back home.

"Where were you, Dad? Why did you take so long? Don't you know that Mom has not had even a drop of water since morning, and now when she is supposed to end her fast you just disappeared." Lalsa was angry. It was the first time in her life when she had sided with her mother and gone against her father.

"Calm down, dear! I told you that I had an urgent meeting," Vijay tried to pacify her.

"No, Dad, it is highly insensitive on your part to ignore Mom today when she was fasting for your long life."

"Okay! Sorry, Kanta! Please forgive me. Now don't delay it further. Let's go upstairs to see the moon and then please eat something." Kanta didn't say anything but she was not convinced in her heart. She had decided to find out the truth once and for all.

Two days later, on Sunday, after having breakfast with Lalsa and Kanta, Vijay left for Nagpur on a business trip at

10:00 a.m. as he had to catch the flight at 12:30 p.m. Kanta had to go to her friend's house, so both of them left home at the same time. Lalsa went to the gym. She decided to have protein shake in the gym café where she saw Dimpy sitting with a sombre face.

"What happened, Dimpy? I have never seen you like this before," Lalsa asked inquisitively. Tears rolled down her cheeks. She wiped the tears immediately and said, "Kunal has stopped talking to me!"

"I thought both of you were going very steady! What happened?"

"Actually, you know he used to come late in the evening to meet me but during the day time I used to feel very lonely and bored. I befriended Gaurav who I met through a common friend. Whenever I felt bored, he would come and take me for a long drive."

"Yesterday, when I was with Gaurav, Kunal called and asked me what I was doing. I lied and said I was at home. He reached my house early to surprise me and saw me stepping out of Gaurav's car with shopping bags in my hands. When we went inside the house, he asked me about him. I told him that he was my cousin. He opened the shopping bag and saw a Burberry bag which Gaurav had gifted me, along with the price tag of thirty-five thousand rupees. Kunal left the house in a rage. I have been calling him since yesterday but he is not picking up the phone."

"But why did you cheat on him?"

"Gaurav is my casual friend, that's all!"

"Then why did you accept such an expensive gift from him?"

"You know, I had always coveted that bag, that's why I couldn't say no to Gaurav," Dimpy said with a wink.

"Although I don't understand your logic of taking the gift from Gaurav but yes, I can understand your pain of being away from Kunal. It is difficult to part with the person you love the most," Lalsa said with moist eyes as she remembered Drishtant. Suddenly, Dimpy's face changed and again she said in a jubilant voice, "But I have to tell you something more."

"What?" Lalsa got confused to see a tremendous change in her mood. With twinkling eyes and naughty smile she continued, "When Kunal left my house I could not tolerate his rejection. I decided to go to his house to make up with him but didn't have a car. I was standing on the road trying to hire a cab, when suddenly a car stopped near me and a very handsome young guy offered to drop me. He seemed to be a sober person. Therefore, I accepted his proposal. He told me that he is working in the Merchant Navy and is based in Bengaluru. He had come to Delhi for three days for some work. He invited me to have coffee with him. I couldn't say no," Dimpy giggled.

"Oh my god! Dimpy, you and your mischievous ways are beyond my understanding! Anyway, my coach must be waiting for me. Let's go now."

Lalsa reached home after her workout. Her mother had not returned till then. She called her but when her mother picked up the phone, she was busy talking to somebody. She hastily told Lalsa that she would talk to her later and disconnected the call. Lalsa was amazed because of her mother's unusual behaviour but decided to wait for her. Kanta came back after an hour. She looked pale and haggard.

"Where were you, Mom? Is everything okay?" Lalsa was worried. Kanta didn't answer, she sat on the chair with a thud. She hid her face in both the hands and started crying loudly. Lalsa sensed that something terrible had happened. She sat down near her, held her by her shoulders and asked, "What happened, Mom? Is everything fine?"

Kanta hugged her and started howling.

"For God's sake Mom, at least tell me what has happened?" Lalsa asked.

"Everything is finished, Lalsa! Your father has destroyed our lives completely. How could he do this to us?"

"But what did he do? Please tell me. You are scaring me!"

"You father has a second wife with two children," Kanta started howling again.

"Are you kidding me, Mom?" asked Lalsa with a pale face.

"No Lalsa, it is true! Your father has been cheating on me for over twenty years now. He has another family."

"But how do you know, Mom? There is surely some misunderstanding." Lalsa's heart didn't want to believe her mother. How could her father who had always treated her like a princess cheat on her and a wife like Kanta!

"I have verified everything on my own." Kanta narrated the incident as she sobbed helplessly.

In the morning, when Vijay left for Nagpur, Kanta followed him in a cab which was already waiting for her outside the house. He didn't go to the airport but went to a house in Patel Nagar. She had her cab parked at a distance and kept waiting for Vijay to come out. About an hour and a half later, Vijay left the house. She got out of the cab and went to the man ironing clothes under a shed in front of that house.

Kanta asked him, "Tell me *bhaiya*, do you come here every day?"

"Yes, Madam" he answered.

"Actually, I am also going to shift into this colony, that's why I am asking you because I may need your services."

"Sure, Madam! You give me your address I will pick your clothes every morning and after ironing them, I will return the clothes on the same evening."

"Okay, *bhaiya*! Tell me, do you know the person who just came out of this house because I think he is my husband's friend but I am not sure. Do you know him?" Kanta asked him.

"Yes, yes! He is Khanna *sahib*. He lives here with his wife and two children."

Kanta got the shock of her life. She felt as if she would fall down on the road. But she gathered herself and decided to go inside the house and check out for herself. She rang the door bell. A lady of Kanta's age opened the door. After looking at Kanta's face, she got nervous and tried to close the door but Kanta stood between the door and said sternly, "I want to talk to you."

"But I don't want to talk," the lady answered.

"Why don't you want to talk to me? Why are you afraid of me?" Kanta asked her as she entered the house. She was shocked to see that the furniture of the drawing room was exactly the same as that of her drawing room.

"Oh my god! Did Vijay get all these things for you?" Kanta asked her angrily.

The lady didn't answer. Kanta walked into the bedrooms also. She was stunned to see that everything from the bed to the dining table, refrigerator and the television –was identical. She saw pictures of that lady, Vijay and two children posing as a happy family on the walls of that house.

She asked her, "Tell me, are you my husband's keep?"

"No, I am his wife. We had a court marriage. I am his wife," she repeated.

"Did you know that he is already married to me?"

"Yes! He doesn't hide anything from me," the lady answered in a stinging voice.

"Who are you? What is your name?"

"I am Maninder. My brothers told you about Vijay's relationship with me but even then you married him."

Kanta was crestfallen. "But Vijay denied everything! He said that he didn't have any relationship with you and your brothers were forcing him to marry you."

"Had it been the truth, he wouldn't have married me later."

"Why didn't you meet me and tell me the truth?"

"Because my brothers took me back to Patiala forcefully. I ran away from Patiala after a month and came back. By then, he had already married you."

"Then why did you marry a married man?"

"I was pregnant with his child. By that time, it was too late to get my child aborted. Had I told my brothers about my pregnancy, they would have killed me and Vijay. Therefore, I requested Vijay to marry me for the sake of my child."

"But your marriage is invalid!"

"No, it is not because he converted to Islam before marrying me which allows a man to have more than one wife."

Lalsa fell short of words after hearing the entire episode. Kanta started crying bitterly once again. "I didn't know what to say. I knew that it was Vijay's fault. Maninder was not answerable to me. It was he who had cheated on us. For me, the whole world came to an end. I have been sharing my man unknowingly, with another woman, for so many years. The only man to whom I had devoted my whole life has been very conveniently cheating on me since so many years. I felt like ending my life but the thought of you stopped me from taking that extreme step."

"Is she the same lady about whom you told me that day?"asked Lalsa.

"Yes, she is the one with whom your father had had a relationship before our marriage also. He is a cheat! He lied to me and his family that he didn't have any relationship with her. Can you believe he has a daughter your age or maybe a little older than you and a boy also from that lady?" Kanta seemed devastated.

Lalsa didn't know how to pacify her mother. She herself was completely heartbroken. She had always considered herself as the princess of her house for whom her father could go to any extent. But suddenly she came to know that she was sharing her father with two other children who had as much right as she had on her father.

She told herself that it was not the right time to ponder over her loss. She decided to face the situation bravely and be there for her mother whose grief was much greater than hers. She fetched a glass of water and after making her mother drink some water, she placed her mother's head on her lap and started pressing it gently. She was doing exactly what her mother always did for her whenever she was under stress or unwell.

Two hours later, Vijay came home. Kanta locked the room and refused to talk to him. He looked very tense. Lalsa stood in front of him. Looking directly in his eyes she said, "Why, Dad? Why did you do this to us? My mother didn't deserve this from you. What was her fault? Why did you cheat on us?" Lalsa asked in a firm and hurtful tone.

Vijay could feel his daughter's pain. He hugged her and started crying. Lalsa pushed away his hands from her neck and distanced herself from her father. With a straight face, she asked again, "Tell me, Dad! What was our fault? Why did you cheat on us?"

"Lalsa, you may not be able to understand it. I didn't do anything deliberately. All my life, I have loved one woman and that is Kanta. But in everyone's life, there are some uncontrollable weak moments. I had one such moment with Maninder for which I had to pay with my whole life. I didn't want to marry her but she was pregnant. Had I not accepted her at that time, she would have committed suicide. My conscience didn't allow me to do that. I couldn't have washed my hands off my responsibility. That's why I married her. I didn't take that step for my pleasure but to perform my duty. Tell me, Lalsa what else I could have done?"

"Dad, don't try to cut such a sorry figure. You have cheated on a lady with whom you had a relationship of five years before marriage and twenty years after marriage. But you didn't bother to tell her anything about the other woman."

"I am sorry, Lalsa. But whatever happened in the past cannot be undone. Tell me, what should I do to placate your mother?"

"Dad, in this life you cannot do anything to pacify my mother. Anyway, I think today you should go to that lady, as we are not in a state of mind to bear you in this house."

"No, Lalsa don't talk like this. I love you so much!"

"Dad, it is my request, you please go. I have to look after my mother who is in a deplorable condition right now. I will call you in a day or two, till then please don't bother us." Lalsa said rudely and left the room.

Vijay left the house and Lalsa forcefully made her mother drink some milk but she herself didn't eat anything.

That night, she slept with her mother. The whole night she could hear her mother sobbing till she caught some sleep early in the morning. The same night, she again got an international call and somebody muttered, "I love you! I love you! I love you!"

She was sure that this was some known person who didn't want to disclose his identity.

27

Heartbroken Lalsa

It was difficult to believe that a doting father like Vijay was a cheat. She wanted to run away from the house. The first thing she did in the morning was to pick up her gym bag and head out for the gym. She was the first one to be there. She started with the treadmill which faced the tinted glass of the doctor's office.

Reminiscences of her childhood began to haunt her. She wondered how her father who would not take even small decisions of his life without his daughter's approval, had hidden such a matter from her which would have such a huge impact on their lives. She still remembered the time when she was only twelve years old and her father's car was stolen. Her father had to buy a new car as soon as possible but he waited for a whole month to let his daughter come back home for the holidays and choose a car for him. Her mother had tried to convince him that she was too small to make such a decision but her father had been adamant that he would buy a new car chosen only by Lalsa. He always made her feel very special during her stay in Delhi. He would always wait for her to have breakfast with him. Every Sunday, her father, if not away on business trip would make it a point to take her out for lunch and spend his whole afternoon with his family. They treated Sunday lunch as a family lunch.

One morning, she gave a surprise to her father by preparing breakfast for him and served it to him in a very fine manner, with flowers decorating the tray. Her father was overwhelmed by her gesture. He hugged her with tearful eyes and planted a kiss on her forehead and said, "My little princess has grown up!" In the evening he bought a pair of beautiful earrings in appreciation of her gesture. Vijay had always been a very affectionate person towards Lalsa and her mother. He never gave any reason to his family to be annoyed or suspicious. She never ever dreamt that he was looking after a second family.

Her mother's aggrieved face flashed in front of her. It seemed as if her life had come to a standstill. Resentment against her father began to build up in her heart. She didn't realise that she had started running at a very high speed on the treadmill because of her anger. Tears rolled down her cheeks but without wiping them off, she continued running at a very fast pace. Suddenly a helper came to her and said,"Madam, doctor sir is calling you urgently."

Lalsa stopped the treadmill and asked angrily, "Why?" She couldn't hide her irritation.

"I don't know, Ma'am!" the helper was bewildered because of her unwarranted rudeness. She wiped her face with a towel and went to the doctor's room.

"Come, come! Please come! Have a seat," he said gently. When Lalsa settled in the chair, he offered her a glass of water.

Lalsa sipped the water and asked, "Yes, doctor?"

"Lalsa, are you alright?"

"Yes, doctor!" said Lalsa while looking down.

"I have always seen you composed but today it is different. Can I help you?" Lalsa wanted to control herself but she was too vulnerable to hide her tears. Ultimately, she broke down. She covered her face with both her hands and cried. He got up from his seat and came near her. He put his warm and soothing hand on her shoulder and said, "Please calm down! Calm down, please!"

"I am fine doctor!" Lalsa tried to gather herself. She did not want to cry in front of the doctor.

"Listen, Lalsa. Life is like a roller coaster ride. You have to go through its highs and lows. It can't give you only happiness. You have to bear your share of sorrow also."

"But if your nearest and dearest ones whom you love the most are the reason for your sorrows then it really hurts. Why does it happen with me always?" Lalsa sobbed. She was still trying to overcome the pain of separation with Drishtant when her father gave a fresh, unbearable and unexpected blow to her and her mother.

"Only people that we love deeply have access to our heart. Only they have the power to hurt us the most and cause deep sorrow. It happens to everyone. But it doesn't mean that you should break down or lose hope in relationships. All sorrows come in your life to teach you lessons and help you evolve, grow and learn. Happiness and sorrow, these are two ever-changing states of everyone's life. Both are short lived and bound to change. This phase of your life may be sorrowful but believe me, it will end soon. So be brave and move forward."

"No, it is easy to say such things. You don't know my story. That's why you are telling me to move forward."

"Okay! One day when you feel fine, we will share our stories with each other. Then we will decide who is braver," he said with a fake laugh. Lalsa composed herself and left the room after thanking him. She felt a strange connection with him. When Lalsa came out of the doctor's room, she saw Dimpy in the gym.

"Hey Lalsa, what were you doing with that sexy doctor?"chuckled Dimpy

"Shut up, Dimpy!" Lalsa said in a low voice.

"What happened, Lalsa? Did he say no to your proposal?"

"Stop, Dimpy. It's not funny," Lalsa snubbed Dimpy.

"Why? What happened, anything serious?"

"No. All is well. Okay, see you tomorrow!"

"Why are you leaving so soon?"

"Not feeling too well." Lalsa said and left the gym. She didn't feel like sharing such personal details with Dimpy. She would not be able to understand Lalsa's situation.

For the next one week, Lalsa didn't go to the gym. Dimpy came to her house to meet her. She had one more story to tell her–Kunal didn't call her after that incident so she had replaced him with the Merchant Navy guy. He had extended his leave especially for her. Two days back, when he visited her house in the evening, they boozed a lot and slept with each other. In the morning, that guy woke her up after he heard a commotion in the house. She heard her mother's voice telling the house help to make tea for Dimpy. As usual, her mother was expected to come up after ten minutes with a cup of tea to wake her up. To save herself from the wrath of her parents, she took out her shampoo and threw the opened bottle down the stairs. As desired by Dimpy, when her mother climbed the stairs up, she slipped. Upon hearing the sound of her fall, her father came rushing out and helped her to reach the room to provide her medical aid. Dimpy watched the scene. At that time, nobody was in the lobby. She immediately helped the boy to escape from the house.

Lalsa was astonished to hear the story and wondered how diabolical it was on Dimpy's part to harm her own mother. She decided to change her timings of the gym to avoid her in future.

28

Mother Going Away

On the seventh day, she received a call from the gym. The doctor wanted to talk to her. After he asked her about her health, he asked her to resume the gym as it would help her in releasing the stress. She promised to come the next day.

Next day, she kept the promise and went to the gym. The helper came to tell her that the doctor wanted to see her after she finished her workout. When Lalsa went to see the doctor after her work out, he was busy reading something.

"Good morning, doctor!"

"Oh Lalsa! Very good morning to you too! How are you feeling now?"

"I am good!" she said with a forced smile.

The doctor looked at her for a while. Her eyes clearly manifested her pain.

"Okay! I think I should believe, if you say so. But remember, in case you need a friend for any help, I am always there. You can trust me," the doctor said.

"Thanks, doctor!" said Lalsa with moist eyes. She was touched by his gesture but she could not confide in him about her life so soon. She didn't want to share the episode with Shikha either. She didn't want to tell anybody how her father had betrayed their trust. But it was affecting her mind and body. It was difficult to see her mother's grief. She was totally broken. She had almost stopped eating. There was no end to her tears. It was a very hard time for both mother and daughter as Vijay's infidelity was hard to digest for both of them.

That night, her mother didn't have dinner because of which even Lalsa couldn't eat properly. Her mother got up many times during the night and cried because of which Lalsa could also not sleep that night. She felt that her mother was going away from her and she felt helpless. Her mother was too precious for her to lose.

She still remembered the incessant efforts that her mother made for her admission in the school hostel. Her mother managed to get her admitted to St. Mary's school as a day scholar but she wanted Lalsa to get adjusted in the school hostel as it wasn't possible for her to leave Vijay all alone in Delhi and live with Lalsa. Her mother stayed with her in a hotel. The school was located up a hill. Every day, her mother would go up and down the hill to drop Lalsa at school and pick her up due to which she suffered perpetual pain in her legs.

Three months passed away. In spite of her mother's repeated requests, the Principal didn't give her admission in the school hostel. Her mother lost heart, her health declined. Finally, she wrote a letter to the Principal.

"It was my dream, that if I ever had a girl, I would want to admit her in your school hostel. Eight years back, by God's grace I was blessed with Lalsa, to fulfil that dream. I have been living in Mussoorie with Lalsa, since the last three months, leaving behind my husband, my house and everything in Delhi, hoping that my daughter may finally get admission in your school hostel.

I came here with high hopes and a firm belief in my heart that through you, God may help me in fulfilling my dream. But unfortunately, my daughter didn't get admission in the hostel. My body has stopped coping and my heart has started losing hope with the passage of time. Therefore, I will have to go back with a heavy heart and shattered dreams.

In future if you have a vacancy in the school hostel, then please let me know."

The letter touched the Principal's heart and she finally admitted Lalsa in the school hostel and the day arrived when finally Lalsa had to shift to the school hostel. Lalsa wasn't ready to part with her mother. She clung to her legs and started crying bitterly but Sister Agatha took her in her arms and led her to the dining hall where everyone was having lunch.

She was introduced to a senior girl who lovingly made her sit in her lap. "Oh my god, you are so pretty! My doll come and sit with me," she cooed and kissed her cheeks.

"I am Renuka *didi*! What is your name?"she asked.

"Lalsa," she murmured with sad and suspicious eyes.

"What do you want to eat?" Renuka asked with concern.

Lalsa looked down. Her downturned lips indicated that she could cry any time. Slowly, she murmured, "Nothing."

"Oh my poor baby! Let me feed you," Renuka said and hugged her tight to her chest.

Lalsa felt better and Renuka fed her with her hands. At night, she was made to sleep in the 'baby dorm' where about thirty other little girls were also sleeping.

One more girl was admitted in the hostel on the same day. She was crying incessantly. Lalsa could listen to her sobs till she drifted into sleep.

Next day, when Lalsa's mother came to meet her, she clung to her legs and started howling.

"Mama, take me back! I will not stay here! Please take me back."

"See, you have so many friends here to play with. Believe me, you will have a lot of fun here," her mother replied.

"No, Mama! I won't stay here," said Lalsa adamantly.

"Okay, stay here for a few days! If you don't feel good, then I will take you back home."

Lalsa kept crying loudly. Even a lovely talking doll which her mother had bought for her could not console her. Her mother hugged her tight and planted a number of kisses on her forehead and cheeks.

"Don't worry, baby! I am not going away. I will come to meet you tomorrow also." But Lalsa was not convinced. She wanted to go back home right there and then. Every day, her mother would come to meet her but her brief visit could not pacify Lalsa. She felt like a stranger there and was not ready to mingle with the other girls. She told her mother that if she didn't take her back home, then she would run away from the school. In fact, she had already made the plan.

The school was divided into two parts. The entrance gate of the school opened into a playground with classrooms on each side. The toilet block for the day scholars was near the main gate of the school. All the classrooms and the toilet block were locked in the evening. The hostel was the extended portion of the school, situated behind the classes. There was a big iron gate to separate the hostel from the day school which was locked in the evening.

Finally one evening, she hid herself in the toilet block near the main gate and waited for nightfall to prepare for her escape. Suddenly, she heard a thud shutting off the main gate of the toilet block. She got scared wondering how she would get out through the locked door. Luckily it was only bolted, which she opened with some effort. When she came out of the toilet, it was very dark and to her dismay, a huge lock was put on the main entrance gate of the school. She realised that it was impossible to escape from the school. She decided to go back inside the hostel and tried to open the entrance door of the hostel which was locked from inside. Then she tried to open her classroom but that was also locked. She got very scared and sat near the statue of Mother Mary which was situated in the middle of the playground.

Tears started coursing down her cheeks. After a while the guards and sisters came looking for her. When they saw her sitting alone, they rushed towards her. One of the sisters picked her up in her arms, wiped her tears affectionately and took her to the dining hall where all the sisters and other staff members dined every day.

The staff dining room was completely different from the students dining hall. It was smaller, with comfortable chairs instead of the benches that were placed in the children's dining hall. She could smell the roasted chicken which sharpened her hunger. She was served delicious food and was pampered by all the sisters and teachers. After this incident, she became the darling of everyone and they extended extra care towards her. Gradually, she started enjoying the extra care, love and affection showered on her by everyone and finally dropped the idea of going back home. Her mother would visit Mussoorie at least once a month. That was the time when Lalsa would spend most of her time on Mall Road, where she wanted to stroll every evening but couldn't, as the students were not allowed to go out of the hostel without their guardians.

Her mother always pampered her to her fullest during her stay at Mussoorie. She would take her out for scrumptious lunches at Lal Tibba or at popular restaurants located on Mall Road. She really liked the pastries and softy ice cream available on Mall Road and loved shopping for woollens from the shops nearby. The Tibetian market was their favourite destination from where they would buy night suits and footwear. They would walk to Camel's Back to have tea from small *dhaba*s and loved to eat *puri chana* as brunch which she never got in her hostel as most of the time the students were served rice or bread with vegetables or chicken. Kanta's whole life revolved around Lalsa and her father. She lived for both of them selflessly without any expectations.

Lalsa wondered how her father could be so ruthless to his wife and daughter. Her mother, the person she loved the most was so miserable, yet she could not do anything except watch her in agony.

29

Sympathetic Doctor

In the morning, she decided to go to the gym to get some respite from her grief. When she started cycling, she felt very weak. She sat down on the floor. Her body didn't want to budge an inch. She tried to get up but failed. She asked the helper to call the doctor. The doctor came to see her immediately.

"Doctor, I can't get up!" she said in a feeble voice.

"Okay, give me your hand!" the doctor said while taking her hand. Lalsa got up but suddenly everything seemed very hazy to her. She felt as if her head was spinning and then she collapsed. The doctor picked her up in his arms and took her to his room. When she regained her senses, she found herself on the sofa. The doctor was sitting near her on the chair and a helper was standing with a glass of water in his hand.

"How are you feeling now?" the doctor asked.

"I am feeling very weak, doctor!"

"I understand! Your blood pressure had dropped drastically. Please get up and drink some fruit juice. You will feel much better." The doctor helped her to sit on the sofa. She had fruit juice and she actually felt much better after that.

"But why did this happen to me?" Lalsa asked.

"Only you can tell me the reason. Did you have enough food and sleep yesterday and in the morning?" the doctor asked worriedly. Lalsa didn't answer and looked down.

"I knew it! Why are you killing yourself? Do you think that you are the only one who is facing an adverse situation in your life? Even I have so many problems in my life but I don't pity myself like you do."

Lalsa didn't answer.

"Okay! Let's be friends. I would like to share my story with you and also listen to your story. Would you like to share your problem with me? Even if you don't want to, would you like to meet me anytime somewhere outside the gym for coffee?"

Lalsa couldn't say no. The doctor called for a sandwich and coffee for Lalsa.

"Now, please call somebody from your home to pick you up. You have to eat well and rest properly. Will you do that or should I talk to your parents?" the doctor said authoritatively. Lalsa nodded in affirmation. The doctor accompanied her outside the gym and helped her to get inside the car.

"Listen, *bhaiya*! She is not well, so tell her parents to look after her. Lalsa, take care! I will call you in the evening," said the doctor.

Lalsa felt a very strong and a strange connect with the doctor.

30

The Doctor Has A Past

Days passed by. Vijay visited home everyday in the evening to spend some time with Lalsa and Kanta. But everything had changed. Kanta didn't forgive Vijay, in spite of his repeated apologies. She had completely stopped talking to him. Whatever had to be communicated was communicated through Lalsa. She had stopped wearing jewellery and the clothes given by Vijay. She had a fixed deposit of a few lakhs in her bank which she had saved long back from her own earnings. She began to use that money for her needs. Kanta isolated herself completely. She stopped going to kitty parties and even the family functions after it came to her knowledge that Vijay's brother, his family and friends, everyone knew about his second marriage and only she was kept in the dark. She completely lost her faith in love and relationships. Therefore, gradually she alienated herself from the whole world. She spent most of her time reading religious books or watching devotional television channels. Her health also started deteriorating as she stopped having proper food. It seemed as if she had set out on the path of self-mortification.

Lalsa was also very upset after the revelation of her father's second marriage. Her mother's grief further added to her sorrow. Doctor Sushant became more concerned about her health. He started talking to her briefly every day and Lalsa would also go to his room occasionally for a brief chat over a cup of coffee. Shikha was still in London with Drishtant. There was no one to share her grief. She had not shared anything with the doctor who was trying his best to pacify her without knowing anything. He decided to spend some time with her to know more about her problems. One day, when Lalsa went to the gym, the doctor called her to his room.

"Hi, Lalsa! How are you today?"

"I am fine doctor!" Lalsa said with a brief smile.

"I want to invite you for lunch at my place tomorrow. Will it be possible for you to spare some time?"

"Sure, doctor! Is there any occasion or...?" asked Lalsa.

"Nothing much! I thought we are friends now so I should invite you to lunch."

"Oh, I see! You must have invited some other friends also..." Lalsa asked inquisitively.

"Unfortunately, no. Since long, I have not been in touch with my old friends in Delhi. Therefore, you will be the only guest in my house tomorrow," the doctor said with a sad smile.

"Okay! You text me your address and I will reach there," Lalsa said respectfully. She didn't want to decline his invitation as she was indebted to him for being the only person who gave her unconditional emotional support at the worst time of her life when two of the most important men of her life had shattered her completely.

Next day, Doctor Sushant reached home a little early at as he had invited Lalsa for lunch. He had stopped mingling with his old friends in Delhi but he didn't know why he felt some special connect with Lalsa. He could feel that they shared a relationship of pain. He was sure that she was also undergoing the same kind of pain that he had experienced in his life. He heaved a sigh and picked up the photo album lying in front of him. He flipped the pages and stopped at one photograph–a group photo of college students in which Sushant and Simran, the first love of his life, were holding shields.

It was a photograph of Pulse Festival of All India Institute of Medical Sciences (AIIMS), where he had received an award for the best light music singer and Simran had been awarded the best debater. Sushant paused for a while and then got immersed in reminiscences.

Sushant belonged to Mumbai. He was a single child. He lost his mother when he was ten years old but his father gave his hundred per cent to Sushant. His father was a successful businessman and had a very famous saree shop in Mumbai at Kemps Corner. He would wake up early in the morning to send him to school and join him for lunch at home. After lunch, he would take Sushant along to the shop. There was a small room at the back of the shop where Sushant would study while his father attended to the customers along with the staff. They would occasionally dine at a Chinese restaurant called China Town as Sushant was fond of Chinese food.

Sushant was a very serious and bright student. His father played a major role in his success. During examination days, his father would wake up early morning to make tea and snacks for him. Sushant always felt blessed to have a father who never let him miss his mother.

After he finished his schooling in Mumbai, he moved to Delhi to pursue his MBBS from AIIMS, where he met Simran, who was his batch mate. Only twenty per cent of the batch were girls and she was one of them. Simran was from Hoshiyarpur, where she lived with her grandparents. Her parents had moved to Canada with her autistic brother as they felt that the social set-up there was more friendly and sensitive towards specially abled children. But Simran decided to continue her studies in India as it was her dream to do her MBBS from AIIMS. She was a very sharp, witty, good-looking and a vivacious girl.

Sushant was sober and an introvert because of which he was the most desirable boy amongst the boys. Simran was a bold girl who was very fond of Sushant and enjoyed chaffing him. Sushant liked her at the very first sight but maintained a respectable distance from her because of his shy nature. Simran lived in a junior resident hostel at Masjid Moth, while Sushant lived in his uncle's vacant flat in South Extension, Part II. They always met in a group. Many a time, all of them would sit in the canteen and chat. One day, they were having snacks in the canteen when Simran said, "Hey Sushant, why don't you talk to the girls? Are you scared of us?" At which Sushant blushed and the girls burst out into a hearty laugh. Once, when Sushant was driving back home, he saw Simran on the road waiting for a cab. Sushant offered to drop her at her destination, and she accepted his proposal happily.

"Hope you don't have to go out of your way to drop me!" Simran asked.

"No, it is only two minutes away from my house."

"Where do you stay?"

"I stay in South Extension, Part II only a few minutes away from your hostel."

"Do you belong to Delhi?"

"No! I am from Mumbai. I stay at my uncle's vacant flat. He lives in America."

"I see!"

After that, Sushant frequently dropped Simran at her destination. Sometimes they went to Sarojini Nagar Market together to pick up their day-to-day essential things.

"Why don't you talk to the girls?" Simran asked one day.

"Actually, I am the only son of my parents. My mother belonged to Gujarat and I lost her when I was only ten years old. She had a brother who has two sons. My father is also a single child like me. After my mother's death, there was no young girl in my house or in extended family. I studied in a boys' school and was too engrossed in my studies. Throughout my school days, my father was my best friend. You will not believe but actually I didn't get a chance to mingle with girls. Therefore, I feel a little hesitant." Sushant said with a smile.

"Do you know that all the girls of our institute are crazy about you? They are dying to be friends with you but you just ignore them," Simran said with a chuckle and continued, "Why did you choose to talk to me? I think you like me!" Simran giggled.

"No no, it is not like that!" Sushant tried to clarify.

"Okay okay! Now, tell me, when are you inviting me over for coffee to your house?"

"You can come any time, Simran," Sushant answered. He was thrilled as Simran was the first girl in his life who was so upfront with him. That night, while trying to sleep, he repeated the same moments in his head and realised that he liked Simran.

Simran started visiting his house, mostly on weekends, in the beginning, with a group and later, all alone. Sometimes, she cooked authentic Punjabi dishes for him like *kadi* and *sarson ka saag* which he really relished. Simran was a very vibrant and vivacious girl who had filled his life with beautiful colours of love.

One day, Simran was making coffee for both of them in the kitchen and Sushant was arranging some snacks on the table. He didn't realise but he was singing softly. Simran was standing behind him with two cups of coffee in her hands, staring at him with stunned eyes.

"Oh my god, you sing so well!"

"I was just humming!" Sushant said with a laugh.

"No, you were singing so beautifully. It was a famous Bahadur Shah Zafar's poem "*Na kissi ki ankh ka noor hoon.*" I just loved it! Please Sushant, I want to listen to the full song. Please sing! Please!" Simran pleaded.

"Okay, but don't blame me for any mistake as I am only a bathroom singer!" Sushant said with a smile.

"No problem! Now please start!" Simran insisted.

Sushant sang the song but that was not the only song he sang. He had to sing for the entire evening. Simran would take out lyrics from the Internet and surprisingly Sushant sang all the songs very beautifully. He himself was not aware of his talent.

Simran was overwhelmed by his singing. Before leaving that evening, she said, "Today, I can't resist hugging you." She hugged him tight and said, "You are a wonderful person! You made my day! Thanks!"

Sushant didn't know how to react. For the first time in his life, a girl had hugged him. These were very special moments which passed by in a jiffy, leaving behind a sweet memory to cherish.

Like every year, Pulse Festival was scheduled to be held in September and last for a week. More than 20,000 students from all over India were invited to participate in the festival.

Simran participated actively in the arrangements and dragged along Sushant also who was very happy to spend time with her. Due to her outgoing nature, Simran soon became an integral part of the organising committee. She got involved in the cultural programmes and Sushant helped in organising debates and conferences.

During the festival, Simran participated in the debate competition and won the first prize. She coaxed Sushant to take part in the non-classical music competition and he received the award for the best singer. Both were very happy for each other. They became very popular in the college after the festival and thereafter, no important event was held without their participation.

A long break was approaching. Simran had to go to Canada to meet her parents and Sushant to Mumbai. Both were sad as they had become very close to each other by then. They didn't express their love but in their hearts they knew that they had become indispensable for each other. Simran had to catch a flight at 5:00 in the morning. Sushant volunteered to drop her at the airport.

Simran shifted her luggage to his house after having breakfast. That day, both of them were feeling sad and tired. Simran didn't cook anything for him as she didn't feel like going away from him to the kitchen. They ordered in Chinese food. After they finished lunch, Simran persuaded Sushant to sing songs. All the songs were sad which added to the misery of their separation.

"Will you miss me?"asked Simran in a sad voice.

"Of course! You are my best friend. I will definitely miss you a lot!" Sushant answered.

"Only your best friend?" Simran asked romantically, looking deep into his eyes in search of a truthful answer.

Sushant didn't answer in words but Simran found the answer in his eyes which showed immense love for her. Sushant's shy eyes were more transparent and spoke louder than his words.

They were sitting on the bed. Simran came closer to him. She hugged him tightly and made him lie down on the bed and kept her head on the side of his shoulder. Her hand was repeatedly moving on his chest. Both of them were trying hard to hold their tears back. None of them spoke as they felt no need of words to express their emotions.

"It is time to leave," said Sushant at 1:00 a.m. Suddenly, Simran brought her face near his and kissed him on his lips. "Sushant, won't you kiss me?" Simran asked. Sushant was too confused to react. She brought her lips near his and nudged him with her shoulder. He pecked her on her lips. It was the first time in his life that he had kissed a girl.

"Is this a kiss? Anyway, I expect a better performance when I am back," Simran chuckled and continued, "Don't you worry! Next time, I will give you a live demonstration of a variety of kisses," Simran laughed heartily but Sushant was too bashful to react.

Sushant dropped her off at the airport and went to Mumbai the very next day. There was not a single day when they didn't talk to each other.

Ultimately, the most awaited day approached when they had to go back to Delhi. Both of them decided to reach a day earlier than the other students and spend some time together.

Simran arrived late in the evening and Sushant picked her up from the airport. After they reached home, Simran kissed him. Passion was running very high on both the sides. Being a shy person Sushant tried to hold his emotions back but Simran seemed adamant about breaking all the barriers.

She was bold enough to take the initiative and finally they made love to each other for the first time.

After that night, Simran started spending nights at Sushant's place very often. They got very close to each other, both physically and emotionally. Although, Sushant was still very shy but Simran always helped him shed his inhibitions.

Two years had passed away and their relationship strengthened with each passing day. They decided to talk about their relationship to their parents as they were sure that they would not be able to marry anyone else. But destiny had other plans. One day, Simran received a call from Canada that her father had met with an accident and died on the spot. She had to rush immediately to Canada.

That was the last time Sushant saw her. He didn't imagine in his wildest dream that he would never meet her again. Simran called Sushant every day. Her family was going through a very tough phase. She had to take care of her father's business as well as her autistic brother and a heartbroken mother. With the passage of time, she realised that she would not be able to return to India to pursue her studies. There was no other bread winner for her family or to take care of her autistic brother who used to get violent sometimes. She decided to discontinue her studies and told Sushant that it would not be possible for her to marry him and settle down in India, leaving behind her mother and brother who were totally dependent on her. Sushant couldn't say anything to her because he didn't have means to support Simran's family in India as he himself was dependent on his father for the finances.

Suddenly, the door bell rang and Sushant drifted away from his past. He realised that it was 1:30 p.m. and Lalsa was at the door. Both of them had lunch together. While having lunch Lalsa asked inquisitively, "If you don't mind, may I know why are you still single? Why didn't you marry anyone?" Sushant kept quiet for a while and then answered with a smile, "Actually, I had two women in my life. Yet I am alone."

"Both of them have left me forever," Sushant said sadly.

"But why? Where are they now?" Lalsa was eager to know the story of Sushant's life.

"Please tell me what happened? Why did they leave a person like you?"

Sushant thought that Lalsa was too young to understand his circumstances, hence, he decided to tell her a brief story of his life. He told her about his parents and then about Simran.

"We were batch mates and loved each other but she had to leave me because her father passed away and she had to move to Canada where her mother and an autistic brother lived. She is the only one to take care of them. Therefore, she decided to discontinue her studies and settle in Canada permanently. She married someone else in Canada who now lives with her family. "

"Oh no!" Lalsa said with disappointment. "But what happened to the second one?" She asked further.

"I married Resham but after one year, we separated."

"Why?"

"There was a total lack of compatibility. She was a perfect wife but I was imperfect for her as I couldn't give Simran's place to Resham."

Lalsa felt sad for Sushant.

"Look at my destiny, the person whom I loved settled down with someone else and because of her I could not love the person who loved and cared for me. I feel very guilty towards Resham. She has not remarried anyone. We have separated but still she calls me every day. I think I am destined to live without love," Sushant said with a painful smile.

"No, don't say that, doctor! At least you have people around who still care for you. You are still liked by Resham and I am sure Simran, too, thinks of you fondly. But in my case, the love of my life left me forever and my own father also ditched me and my mother."

She narrated her whole story to Sushant who did not have enough words to console her. He knew that it was very difficult to handle deception and rejection from your loved ones at such a tender age. In an attempt to change the topic, he said, "Okay, now no more sad stories! Let's have dessert."

31

Doctor is a Dear Friend

After that lunch at Sushant's house, Lalsa and Sushant became good friends. Slowly and gradually, Lalsa's dependence on him increased. Whether it was about her mother's diet or medicines or her own little problems, Sushant had a piece of advice for every issue in her life. Lalsa also filled a void in Sushant's lonely life. She was like his protégé who found solace in his company. They would talk every day and share everything with each other.

Vijay didn't miss a single as far as visiting Lalsa and her mother went. Lalsa, although angry with him, felt sorry for him. The most respected and cheerful person of the family whose presence always brought happiness around suddenly looked forlorn. He was like an uninvited guest whom nobody wanted to welcome. He had been a star of not only in his family but also for his friends and extended family because of his amicable nature. There were innumerable accounts of his mischief that his friends and family often discussed at gatherings.

Lalsa distinctively remembered one incident when she had come to Delhi to spend her vacations. One of her uncles, Naresh, had also come from Punjab on a business trip.

He was very fond of his hair and always kept a small comb in his pocket to set his hair. He took great care of his hair.

One morning, Vijay was sitting with Lalsa in the lobby. He was reading the newspaper and sipping his tea. Naresh went to the bathroom to take a bath. Vijay looked at him from the corner of his eyes and smiled.

"Lalsa, after a while you will see a miracle." Vijay said with a mischievous smile while sipping tea.

"Why? Are you going to do something with uncle?" Lalsa asked with suspicion.

"Just wait for some time!" Vijay said with a chuckle while turning the page of the newspaper.

"No no, please tell me, Dad! I hope you will not offend him."

"He is a cousin as well as my childhood friend, so I have every right to play games with him!" Vijay said smilingly while shrugging his shoulders. After fifteen minutes, Naresh came out of the bathroom. Everything seemed to be fine. He went to his room to get ready. Lalsa looked at her father's face questioningly. Vijay nodded with closed eyes and said, "Don't get impatient, baby. Wait for ten minutes."

Lalsa's heart fluttered with excitement and fear. "Dad, please stop otherwise I will tell Mom." Lalsa threatened Vijay.

"Dear baby, now even God can't help him," Vijay said in a serious tone as he raised his hands towards the sky. He was right! After ten minutes, Naresh came out of the room looking completely frightened.

"See, Vijay what is happening with my hair. Whenever I comb, I loose a bunch of hair," He seemed to be extremely shocked. Lalsa was not ready to believe that her father was behind his uncle's hair fall.

"Oh my god!" Vijay said in a worried tone.

"How is it possible? Did it happen with you earlier also?" he continued with the same concern.

"No, never!" Naresh was disheartened.

"Now, I understand why this has happened to you. Do you remember you got yourself tonsured after your father's death because it is your family tradition to get yourself tonsured after a parent's death?"

"Yes!" Naresh said with a nod.

"But you didn't shave your hair after your mother's death last month, so may be your mother's soul is offended by you. But don't worry, it will grow back soon." Vijay said with a fake veneer of concern on his face.

Naresh Uncle was a simple man and readily believed Vijay's lie. Vijay told Lalsa that he had replaced Naresh's hair conditioner with hair removal cream. Lalsa felt very bad over the incident. She could never think of hurting someone for her own entertainment. The poor fellow was told about the truth after three months when his scalp had become hairy once again. In family gatherings, that incident was remembered and laughed at over and over again. But now, Vijay's face had lost the sheen of self-confidence. Nobody could imagine that he'd once had such a crazy sense of humour.

Sushant was the only person who brought some happiness in Lalsa's life. Sushant took her out for lunch also. Her ailing mother noticed that she was talking to a man almost every day. One day, Sushant told Lalsa that his ex-wife Resham wanted to come to Delhi to meet him but he was not ready to meet her because of his guilt. Lalsa advised him to not disappoint her and allow her to meet him. But Sushant told her that he needed some time before he met her again.

Amidst all this, Lalsa came down with a very high fever but she had no one to attend to her. Her father was out of station, her mother was too weak to look after someone and her attendant had also taken leave that day. It was 9:00 at night when Lalsa suddenly started to tremble with a high fever. She had severe body ache and the temperature shot up to 104 degrees. She took medicines but none of the medicines worked. Finally, she called Sushant at 11:00 p.m. He sounded half asleep. After he realised how serious was Lalsa's condition, he immediately rushed to Lalsa's house.

Lalsa's condition deteriorated further. She wailed in pain. He immediately gave her some injections and told her house help to bring cold water and cotton. Then he started putting cold compresses on her forehead. Her temperature came down but she too weak to be left alone with a sick mother. Sushant decided to spend the night at her house as he feared that she may need him any time.

Lalsa's mother came to see her. The doctor was sitting on the chair, holding Lalsa's hand. After she inquired about her health from the doctor, she touched Lalsa's forehead with her hand and left the room without saying anything.

Lalsa's condition was finally under control after some time. She pleaded with Sushant to leave but he refused to leave. Lalsa slept after some time. Sushant also grabbed a few hours of sleep on the sofa in Lalsa's room. He left her house at 6:00 a.m.

Sushant returned at lunch time to see her again. Lalsa was much better. She insisted that the doctor have lunch with her. Sushant expressed his desire to meet her mother. Lalsa took him to her mother's room. Kanta was lying on the bed with her back towards the door.

"Mom! Look, who has come to meet you." Kanta opened her eyes lazily and got up to sit.

"No, Aunty don't bother. Please keep lying!" Sushant said softly.

But Kanta didn't listen. She sat on the bed and asked, "You had come last night also, but sorry I didn't recognise you!"

"Mom, he is Doctor Sushant. He has a clinic in Punjabi Bagh and also owns the gym where I go every day. He saved my life last night. I was so sick, Mom. Had he not been there, I would have died."

"Don't talk like this!" Sushant interrupted immediately.

"You talk to him, Mom. Meanwhile, I will get fresh and tell Ramu *bhaiya* to lay the table." Lalsa said and left the room.

"Are you the one with whom Lalsa talks every day on phone?" Kanta inquired.

"Yes, Aunty, we are friends!" Sushant answered.

"How can you be friends? She is much younger than you! Had you married a little earlier, you would have had a daughter of her age!" Kanta said agitatedly. Sushant was taken aback. He could read between the lines and understood that Kanta was suspecting that they were having an affair.

"Yes, Aunty, you are absolutely right," Sushant said respectfully.

"I hope you keep this in mind forever," Kanta said with a sting in her voice.

"Sure, Aunty!" Sushant felt embarrassed. Lalsa came back with a cold drink in her hand.

"Now, you can sit in the drawing room as I need to take rest." Kanta said rudely.

After returning from Lalsa's house, Sushant introspected on his relationship with Lalsa. He realised that unintentionally he had become very close to Lalsa.

They had started speaking to each other on the phone about five to six times every day. He had developed a platonic relationship with her. Lalsa's mother may have noticed their proximity. Thinking that they might be having an affair, she had disapproved of their closeness because of their age gap. Sushant decided to maintain a distance with Lalsa in future.

Suddenly, he realised he had a missed called from Resham while he was at Lalsa's house. When he called her back, she told him that she was visiting Delhi over the next weekend to spend few days with her cousin, and she would like to visit him too.

Sushant couldn't say no as he had no reason to shun her. She had always cooperated to make their married life a success. After their divorce, she had not married anyone else in spite of tremendous pressure from her parents. He had very high regard for her.

32

Loses Mother

Sushant deliberately reduced the number of calls to Lalsa. Lalsa didn't notice the change as Shikha was back from London to fill the void in her life. As usual, Lalsa shared everything with Shikha. She was also astonished to know the truth about Lalsa's father. She tried her best to keep her cheerful with gossip on her friends and by taking her out to watch movies, having lunches and going for a swim to Roshnara Club. Lalsa was still trying to recover from the shock her father had given them but her mother was not able to overcome the grief of the biggest betrayal of her life by her own husband. She was getting weaker by the day. She had stopped eating and drinking. As a result, she had lost about ten kilos.

Vijay called the doctor home twice but Kanta refused to get her check up done. He arranged for a personal attendant for Kanta but she refused to let her touch her or accept her services. Every day, Lalsa tried hard to make her eat as much as possible but she seldom ate anything. She stopped talking to everyone, even to Lalsa.

Then one day, in the middle of the night, Lalsa noticed that her mother was semi-conscious and had stopped reacting to her questions. She called up her father to apprise him of her condition. Her father told her that he would reach immediately to shift her to a hospital. When her father reached, Kanta had already started gasping for breath. He called for the doctor and the ambulance. Before they could shift her in the ambulance or give her any medical aid, she suffered a massive cardiac arrest and passed away.

It was a severe blow for Lalsa. She had lost the dearest and closest person of her life who had loved her more than her own life. Lalsa was totally shattered. By the evening, all her close relatives like her uncle and her aunts from Punjab and Mumbai reached their house.

Shikha and her mother were of great help. They visited her house every day and helped her in arranging everything for the guests and performing all the rites and rituals. Sushant also visited her house everyday but maintained a reasonable distance from Lalsa as he didn't want her relatives to unnecessarily assume anything about Lalsa and him.

When all the relatives left, her uncle and Nidhi asked her to accompany them to Mumbai for few days but Lalsa refused, saying that the house was in total mess and she needed some time to set everything in order. She didn't tell them about her father's second marriage.

After her uncle and Nidhi left, Vijay said, "Lalsa after your mother's death, I will not be able to stay in this house. I want you to shift to my second house and live with your brother and sister. Maninder is a nice lady. She will look after you as your own mother."

"Dad, please! Nobody can replace my mother. My mother died because of that woman and you are suggesting that I accept her as my mother? You had two wives so you are not bothered because you still have one, but I had only one mother who has gone forever and no one can ever take her place."

"Then tell me what to do? I can't leave all of them and stay here."

No problem, Dad! My mother has gone, I will think that my father has also gone with her. You please don't worry about me. I can live alone," Lalsa retorted.

"You are too young to live alone."

"Okay then, I will live somewhere as a paying guest."

"Lalsa, at least consider the reputation of our family. What would people say?"

"When you were having two families simultaneously, did people say anything to you? You had a loving wife. Even then you married another woman? Did anybody ask you this question? Why would they say anything now? Please don't worry about anyone, just enjoy with your happy family," Lalsa quipped.

"You are too young to understand, Lalsa. But I will tell you the reason. You don't know about the circumstances in which I married Maninder. After marriage, there was not even a single day when my conscience didn't prick me for cheating on you and your mother. I wanted to get rid of Maninder but her complete surrender and selfless love didn't let me leave her. Maninder married me without laying down any conditions. She knew that she was going to be my second wife but she didn't mind. She was ready to pay any price just to be with me. Every man has an ego–he wants to be the leader of his house where he should take the lead and everyone else should follow him and she let me enjoy that status. She never questioned or challenged my decisions. She always walked an extra mile to make me happy. Your mother loved me but she always ruled the house and I followed her commands. But I swear to God, Lalsa, I love you the most in this world."

"It means you needed a housekeeper, not a wife. You followed my mother's commands because of your own guilt. Don't try to justify your misdeeds with such lame excuses, Dad!" Lalsa said furiously and locked herself in her room. She was adamant about not going to her stepmother's house.

In the evening, when her father had gone out, she called up Shikha asking her to come over. Shikha was at a family function at that time but she promised that she would come at night. Lalsa was too restless to wait till the night. She desperately needed a shoulder to cry on. She called Sushant and requested him to meet her urgently. Sushant reached her house immediately.

"Tell me Lalsa, how can I help you?" he asked affectionately.

"Doctor, without considering my emotions my father wants me to move into my stepmother's house. Tell me how can I shift there?" Lalsa sniffled. Sushant sat near her and held her hand.

"Don't be disheartened, Lalsa! I understand your feelings but you can't live alone. If you don't go to that house, then your father should shift to this house."

"He said that after my mother's death, he would not be able to stay here anymore."

"I understand Lalsa that the ghosts of his past would always chase him and the guilt of betrayal would always prick his heart. In such circumstances, living in this house would further aggravate his problems," Sushant said in concerned voice.

"But what about my problems? How can I live with the woman who killed my mother? Why should I suffer? It is his fault and he should be prepared to suffer the consequences."

"You are right. But if he doesn't cooperate, then what will you do, Lalsa?"

"I want to shift to a women's hostel but he is not ready to cooperate with that either. I may marry any Tom, Dick or Harry but would not shift to my stepmother's house," Lalsa said with anguish.

"What rubbish! You can't spoil your whole life by marrying someone in haste."

Lalsa felt hopeless and helpless. She was in a frenzy. Suddenly, she held Sushant's hand with both her hands and said, "Doctor, please marry me! Please! I will not expect anything from you and will always keep you happy! But please save me from that witch," Lalsa started howling. Sushant's eyes moistened. He hugged her affectionately. As he patted her head he said, "Lalsa, you are very special and dear to me. Whosoever will marry you, will be the luckiest person on earth. But I am a total misfit for you. You are too young to marry me. I don't want you to ruin your life because of your impetuous decision. Give me some time to find out a solution and you also think patiently before taking any hasty decision. Maybe you can shift to the college hostel and complete your studies as well. Please understand you are too young to discontinue your studies and get married," Sushant said warmly. He went to the kitchen and got a glass of water for Lalsa. After pacifying her, he said, "I think before your father comes, I should leave Lalsa."

Sushant left her house with a heavy heart. He was very fond of Lalsa. After Simran and Resham, she was the one who had touched and soothed his loveless, lonely heart with her innocent and selfless affection. But he didn't want to destroy her life like Resham's by marrying her. He felt miserable for being unable to extend any help to Lalsa.

Later in the evening, Lalsa called Sanya to share her agony. Sanya was very sad to hear about Lalsa's mother's sudden demise. She had seen her closely since her childhood and shared her mother's affection, being Lalsa's closest friend. She never forgot to bring a gift and home-made food for Sanya during her visit to Mussoorie. Sanya told Lalsa that she was coming to India after a few days and before going to her own house in Mumbai, she would meet Lalsa in Delhi. Lalsa told her that she didn't want to go to her father's second wife's house as she was responsible for her mother's untimely death. Sanya understood her agony. She suggested Lalsa get admission in her dream college in London to pursue her studies. She told Lalsa that her present college Pearl Academy has an affiliation with London College of Fashion Designing, where the next session was going to start after one month, in September. She said that it would not be a problem for a bright student like Lalsa to get admission in London, where she could stay with Sanya and share her studio apartment. She suggested that Lalsa should discuss the proposal with her father. Lalsa was hopeful of getting a nod from her father as he had promised her earlier to let her study in London.

Vijay came back in the evening. Lalsa expressed her will to go to London for further studies after one month. Her father agreed to send her to London on the condition that she immediately shift to his second house and spend a few days there. He said that he was worried about her future. After Kanta's death, he was scared to think that if something were to happen to him then Lalsa would be left alone in this world. In that case, if she agreed to maintain a cordial relationship with his second wife and children, then at least she would have a complete family around her. Lalsa didn't accept his proposal. She was not ready to meet her father's second family.

Shikha came in the evening to see Lalsa. Vijay knew that Lalsa was very close to Shikha and she was the only one who could convince her to accept his proposal. He decided to take her help. He called her to his room.

"Shikha, you are aware of all the circumstances. I need your help. You please convince Lalsa to shift with me to my second house," Vijay pleaded.

"But Uncle, Lalsa is not at all ready to go there. She is completely shattered. Therefore, I would request you to not pressurise her to take any hasty step for which we may have to repent later for the rest of our lives."

"What do you mean?" Vijay sputtered.

"Yes Uncle, I am not trying to frighten you but this is the truth. She is extremely vulnerable right now. She may take an extreme step to avoid your second house. I request you to give her some time to stabilise and then take any decision."

"But what should I do now? It is very difficult for me to spend even a single night in this house. I would go mad!" Vijay looked frightened.

"You don't worry, Uncle! I will take her to my house for a few days. It will be a change for her and also give her some time to introspect," Shikha tried to reassure Vijay.

"Okay! But try to convince her as soon as possible," Vijay felt relieved.

Lalsa agreed to shift to Shikha's house the next day. Lalsa felt comfort in her company and could trust her implicitly. She thought of Sushant and called him to tell him about the recent developments including the possibility of shifting to London for her studies. She also told him that she was shifting to Shikha's house for a few days. He was happy with her for the decision she had taken.

33

Love is Back

It was a Friday night when Sushant got a call from Resham who told him that she had reached Delhi and wanted to see him. Sushant invited her for lunch next day at his house as it was the only time he was relatively free from his hectic schedule. That night, Sushant could not sleep properly. He could not stop himself from revisiting the time spent with Resham.

Sushant was left heartbroken after the end of his love story with Simran, who married an Indian boy of her community based in Canada, nearly two years after her mother's persistence. Her husband shifted to Simran's house as he was alone in Canada and his whole family lived in Punjab. After her wedding, Simran stopped calling Sushant as she wanted to adjust in her married life and forget about her first love.

Sushant completed his MBBS and decided to practise independently. He opened his clinic in Mumbai and started doing well. His father persuaded him to get married to a girl, who was from Pune. Her name was Resham and she belonged to an affluent family. Sushant accepted the proposal as he didn't want to hurt his father's sentiments. His father had always stood like a wall for Sushant through everything. Resham was a very mature and understanding girl. She was an excellent homemaker and a loving wife. But misfortune didn't stop following Sushant.

On the first night of their marriage, Sushant was not able to have a physical relationship with Resham. They waited for the next night but again failed. Sushant discussed with his friends who told him that there was nothing unusual in their case, as many times it happens with men, especially with those who had never had any physical relationship with any other girl before getting married. Sushant could not tell his friends that he'd had a physical relationship with Simran for two years in the past but even then he had faced some problems.

Three months passed by but they didn't succeed in consummating the marriage. Resham handled everything patiently. She encouraged him not to panic and told him to wait for sometime. Meanwhile, they became great friends. Like Sushant, she was also fond of music. They would have a glass of wine every evening and enjoy the music. Resham was very fond of watching movies. Sushant would try to take her out for movies. There were times, when the two of them would watch movies back-to-back on Sundays. Resham was a very good companion but Simran was still alive in his heart.

Sushant was himself a doctor but even then he decided to consult a sexologist. Both of them went to see the doctor. After the doctor had examined Sushant, the doctor said that he was completely normal. They didn't know how to handle the problem. Resham went to a tantrik with a friend without telling Sushant. The tantrik who told her to meet him alone as he would teach her practically how to seduce her husband.

Resham understood that he wanted to assault her. She got nervous and told everything to Sushant who was devastated to learn of the incident. He understood that like every human being, she had physical desires which he was unable to fulfil. He told her to divorce him but Resham refused.

They consulted a psychologist. He listened to their stories and told each of them to meet him separately on the next visit. During their next visit, he asked Sushant whether he'd had a physical relationship with any girl earlier in his life. Sushant narrated his whole love story. The doctor told him that he was not able to consummate his marriage because he was obsessed with Simran and was finding it difficult to have a physical relationship with his wife. He told him to forget the past and move forward. He told Resham to play a more proactive role. Both of them tried to abide by the doctor's instructions. In spite of tireless joint efforts, they failed to consummate their marriage.

One year passed by. It was their wedding anniversary and Resham's parents were in town. When her parents found out about their marriage through Resham's friend, they forcefully took her back and applied for a divorce. She wanted to come back to Sushant but he dissuaded her and told her to move on. The court granted them divorce in a year's time and Sushant was again left alone. Resham still loved him and maintained regular communication with Sushant. She called him up every day to know about his well-being. Sushant felt embarrassed at the thought of seeing her after so long. He always held himself responsible for the incomplete and unhappy life of Resham. She could not move on in her life without him.

Next day, Sushant gave instructions to his house help to cook food for Resham also and then went to the gym and his clinic. When he reached back his home Resham was already there. She was in his bedroom busy settling his completely messed up cupboard.

"Hey, Resham! How are you and what are you doing with my cupboard?" Sushant asked laughingly.

"I am good but you are just the same disorganised person!" Resham answered amusedly. Sushant couldn't miss the sadness of her eyes.

"Don't behave like a nagging wife!" Sushant said with a smile.

"No, I am not being a nagging wife. I am behaving like a concerned friend," Resham got embarrassed.

"If you are so concerned about me, then why did you leave me alone?" Sushant quipped with a sad smile. Resham's hands trembled and eyes moistened. Sushant realised his mistake. To change the topic, he said hurriedly, "Anyway, now let's have lunch. I am very hungry!"

Both proceeded towards the dining table. Looking at the food, Resham screamed with excitement, "Oh my god, you still remember my favourite dishes! Dry *masala* chicken, *rajma* rice and *bhindi*!"

"Yes, because after you left I didn't allow anyone else to enter in my life to erase your memories," Sushant said laughingly.

"Who knows it better than me that you don't erase your memories?" Resham looked deep into his eyes," and continued, "So how is Simran? Any news of her?"

"No!"

"At least talk to her and tell her that she ruined your life. You have not been able to move on in your life because of the baggage of her memories," Resham said.

"But it is not her fault. She left me because of her family compulsions. The fault lies within my heart which doesn't realise the reality and refuses to move on."

"I insist that you talk to her or go to Canada and meet her once. Maybe then you will understand the reality. The problem with you is that you separated from her suddenly. Everything happened so quickly that your mind didn't register the reality. Once you see her happy and busy with her family, then you will also be ready to move on in life. Who knows, you may win her back once again! In both the cases, it will be a win-win situation for you."

"Okay, I will think about it. But why didn't you move on? Are you still in love with me?" Sushant said with a chuckle. Resham could feel the hollowness of his laughter. She couldn't answer. Her face turned pale because it was true that she still loved him madly.

"Okay, forget everything and let's eat," Sushant said with a smile in order to change the topic. After lunch, Sushant and Resham dispersed as Sushant had appointments in his clinic.

That night, Sushant could not sleep as Resham had delved into his heart and the old memories had resurfaced. He realised that after his divorce with Resham, he had missed her a lot. In fact, he missed Resham more than Simran.

He failed to figure out the reason. He wondered whether it was out of his own guilt or his fondness for Resham. Despite the lack of physical compatibility, he found a true companion in Resham. He never wanted her to go out of his life but after he realised her physical needs, he happily agreed for a divorce.

Simran had left him in a lurch without considering his condition. She didn't even bother to give him a chance to find some way out to be together. She was only concerned about her own family. On the contrary, Resham tried her best to help him overcome his past. He had a lot of respect for Resham. He genuinely wanted her to do well in life.

Next morning, Resham called him up to tell him that she had extended her stay in Delhi. She started coming to Sushant's house everyday to have lunch and dinner with him. Sushant loved her company and in his heart he never wanted her to go back but he was not confident of his own capability of giving her happiness which she deserved. The whole week just flew by and it was Saturday. Resham was supposed to leave on Monday morning.

Resham had bought a shirt for Sushant. She wanted him to wear the shirt and check the size. Sushant went to the bedroom and after wearing the shirt he called Resham inside. He was looking very handsome.

"It is really suiting you!" After a pause she said sadly, "Sushant, can I come for dinner also?"

"Sure Resham! It is your own house and you can come here whenever you want to!"

"It is my house till you don't marry somebody else," Resham murmured with a deep sigh. She seemed to be completely devastated.

"Are you crazy, Resham? There will be no one else after you, that is a promise to you," Sushant held her hand and said affectionately. Tears streamed down Resham's cheeks. She covered her face with both her hands and started sniffling. Sushant hugged her tight to his chest.

"Don't cry, Resham! I am so sorry to ruin your life. Please forgive me. Tell me, what can I do to make you happy?" Sushant asked with teary eyes.

"Sushant, please don't let me go! I tried hard but I can't live without you. I love you truly. I don't want anything but only you and your love. That will be sufficient for me to be happy. Please marry me again, Sushant!"

Sushant could not hold back his tears anymore. Both of them hugged each other and cried together.

"No, Resham, I want to see you happy! Don't ruin your life because of me. I can't see you deprived of happiness. You will find someone else who can keep you happy."

"Listen Sushant, I will never marry anyone else again. You are the first and will be the last man in my life. You are the only one who can make me happy. Please overcome your past, and do something for me and yourself, for once. I love you and I know you love me too!"

"Yes, I...I love you!" Sushant stuttered.

He kissed her frantically and Resham responded passionately too. Sushant locked the room. He pushed her gently on the bed. The room was full of passion. Both of them were caressing and loving each other as if it was the last chance of their life to love each other and be together.

Finally, what never happened in the years of their married life, happened. Both of them cried but these tears were of sheer joy. The tears were cold and soothing. Resham dropped the idea of going back to her parents' house. They decided to apply for the court marriage next day.

34

Lalsa Leaves Home

Lalsa shifted to Shikha's house. All the members of her family tried to comfort Lalsa as much as possible. Especially Vrinda, Shikha's mother was very caring towards her. But Lalsa had become very vulnerable. She would cry very often without any reason. Her legs trembled with nervousness. She had completely lost her confidence. A few months back, she considered herself the apple of her father's eye but suddenly he had become so ruthless that without considering her emotional condition, he was forcing her to live with the family responsible for her mother's death. She felt very lonely. There was no one to love or care for her. She forgot to smile.

She also stopped going to gym but Sushant called her up every day. Sushant inquired about many girls' hostels where Lalsa could stay safely but was not satisfied with any of them. He really wanted to do something for Lalsa but felt completely helpless. One day, he invited Shikha and Lalsa for coffee along with Resham who felt very sad to learn of her story. Sushant tried his best to comfort and cheer her up but she was in a deplorable condition. Sushant didn't know how to help her.

It was morning and Lalsa was getting ready for college when she received a call on her mobile from an unknown number. She didn't take the call but the phone kept ringing. Finally, she picked up and said, "Hello" in an irritated tone. On the other side, she heard a soft voice.

"Hi, Lalsa! Robin this side. How are you?"

Lalsa was taken aback as she never expected Robin to ever call her again.

"Hi, Robin! I am fine! But this is not your number. That's why I didn't take the call. I thought it was a wrong number."

"Yes, this is my temporary number for India and why do you sound different Lalsa? Are you sick?"

"No no, I am fine!" Lalsa said with a fake laughter.

"Actually Lalsa, a few days back, I had a dreadful dream about you. You were crying bitterly and no one was around you. I desperately wanted to talk to you but didn't have the courage to call. I thought you may take it otherwise. Today, when I reached Delhi, I couldn't stop myself. Tell me honestly, is everything okay?"

Lalsa broke down and started sobbing.

"What happened, Lalsa? Can we please meet for a while?" Robin was concerned.

"Okay!" Lalsa said after she calmed down a bit. She felt very lonely and needed her friends who could truly understand the rough patch she was going through. They decided to meet at the same restaurant where they had met the last time.

Robin was astonished to see Lalsa's condition. He immediately held her hand in his hand and asked hurriedly, "What has happened to you, Lalsa? Tell me, please."

"I lost my mother," she said as tears rolled down her face.

"Oh I am so sorry! I know how grave is the grief of losing a parent at this age. But I hope your father is taking good care of you and what about the boy who was in your life?"

Lalsa shared everything with Robin. He was at a loss for words to console her. He realised that the quantum of her problems was far graver than his own problems.

After a pause, he said, "Listen Lalsa, you should know that I still love you and can go to any extent to make you happy. Tell me, how can I help you?"

"Robin, I don't want to live in my stepmother's house."

"Lalsa, it is a matter of a few days now, as you told me you will shortly shift to London and fulfil your dream of studying in London College of Fashion Designing. We will be together once again. I am really excited about seeing you in London. I will be the happiest person to have you back in my life. But if your father changes his mind, then I would feel honoured to bear all the expenses very happily."

"Thanks Robin but my father has already agreed to bear the expenses."

"Lalsa, I have to go back to London tonight but I will come back soon after a few days. Till then you pack your bags and once you are in London, I shall always be at your service." After a pause he said, "If you want, I can transfer some money right now in your account for any emergency."

"No, no!" Lalsa felt embarrassed.

"Don't be formal with me, Lalsa. We are friends. You can return the money afterwards," Robin said gently and kept his hand on hers.

"No, Robin if I need something, I will definitely let you know." Lalsa felt indebted, she knew that her conscience would not allow her to take any favour from Robin but his selfless gesture touched her heart.

"I will tell Sanya to send you all the details about your admission in London College of Fashion Designing. I have heard that they also have some diploma courses of short duration. In case you have to wait for some time to get admission in the next session, you can do one of the diploma courses they offer."

Lalsa felt a bit relieved for the first time after her mother's death. She felt blessed to have a selfless friend like Robin. They had lunch together and then Robin left for the airport. When she reached Shikha's house, Shikha noticed her calm and serenity. Lalsa told her everything. Shikha was full of praise for Robin's generosity and concern.

That evening, Sanya called her up and sent her all the details of the college. She advised her to choose the course and apply for the admission as soon as possible. Lalsa promised to do that.

It was late evening. When Shikha had gone to have a shower and Lalsa was reading a magazine in Shikha's room with her back to the door of the room. Suddenly, she felt a heavy hand on her shoulders. She immediately turned back and stood up with a shock.

35

He is Back

It was Drishtant.

"Lalsa, I am so sorry to hear about your mother's demise," he said.

Tears coursed down Lalsa's cheeks. Drishtant immediately hugged her. Lalsa started howling as if she just wanted to pour out all her in the form of tears on his chest. He didn't stop her from crying and kept patting her head. Drishtant gave her a glass of water lying on the table. Lalsa felt a strange kind of relief.

Shikha laid the dinner in the bedroom but Lalsa didn't feel like eating.

"Come on! Don't behave like a child or I will feed you with my hands!" Drishtant said laughingly. Lalsa also smiled for the first time in the last fifteen days after her mother's death because of Drishtant. They talked till late into the night. Lalsa shared everything about her mother with him. He listened to her patiently. They chatted till early morning and finally decided to sleep at 4 a.m. While Drishtant tried to sleep, he kept thinking about Lalsa and felt very sorry for her. When he left for London, she had a happy family around her but now she was in a miserable condition.

He wondered how he could be so informal with her. Six months ago, they had separated and after that, they hadn't even talked to each other. But when he saw her, everything was wiped off from his mind and he hugged her just the same way he used to, before their break-up. But why didn't Lalsa stop him? He was genuinely at fault as he had misbehaved with her. Had she forgiven him? Did she still love him? With many uneasy questions in his head, he tried to get some sleep. On the other hand, Lalsa's mind was totally blank. After so many days, she slept like a baby that night.

In the morning, when Lalsa woke up, she wondered why she suddenly felt so secure and relieved. Drishtant was the same boy who had misbehaved with her and she had promised herself never to talk to him again in her life. He had not bothered to even apologise to her or call her after their separation. Then why did he hug her and why did she cry on his chest so comfortably for so long without any inhibitions. Why did she allow Drishtant to pat her with those very hands which had mercilessly pushed her out of the car the last time they had met? She wondered whether her present circumstances had made her so vulnerable that she behaved so strangely, or did she still love him?

At the breakfast table, both of them were not as comfortable as they were last night. There could be a possibility that after the emotional outburst last night, they realised that they had gone overboard. Drishtant had everyone engaged with his stories and experiences from London. While talking, he deliberately avoided direct eye contact with her. Lalsa also felt a little uncomfortable. She could understand that Drishtant was also avoiding her because of the same reason. After they finished breakfast, Lalsa and Shikha went to their room. Drishtant also went to his room but couldn't stop himself for long from going near Lalsa. After ten minutes, he went to Shikha's room.

"So Shikha, what is the programme for today?"

"Nothing much, *bhaiya*! Lalsa has become very boring. She is not ready to go anywhere."

"Okay, right now I am going to the factory but in the evening, we will watch some movie."

"No, but I will not go!" Lalsa said.

"Shikha, tell your friend that nobody says no to Drishtant," he said with a broad smile. Shikha laughed loudly and Lalsa also smiled to hear his pet sentence after so long. In the evening, they went to watch a movie. Drishtant didn't sit with Lalsa. She sat on the corner seat, Shikha was in the middle and Drishtant on the third seat. It was a comedy movie which really changed Lalsa's mood. They dined out and came back late at night.

Next day, after Drishtant came back from the factory, he took both of them to watch a play at Kamani Auditorium. He was trying his best to make Lalsa happy. Lalsa was touched by his selfless efforts but still the old connection and comfort were missing. Drishtant avoided any conversation with her whenever she was alone. He always came to her room in the presence of Shikha. Even Lalsa was not very comfortable while talking to Drishtant alone. She was neither sure about her own feelings nor about his feelings towards her. Lalsa's father called her up every day and tried to convince her to come back but each time Lalsa said that she needed more time.

On the seventh day of her stay in Shikha's house, Lalsa's father came to see her. Drishtant had left for the office by then.

"Lalsa, get your stuff and let's go home," Vijay said softly.

"Which home are you talking about, Dad?" she said bitterly.

His father looked at her for a while with sad eyes and said, "You know dear, we have only one home now, where your brother and sister are waiting for you."

"No, Dad! I don't have any brother or sister. I will not go there," Lalsa was adamant.

"Then, where do you want to go?" Vijay was harsh.

"I want to go to London next month and till then, I can go to Mumbai and stay with Uncle or I can shift to a guest house."

"I can't allow you to go anywhere."

"I will die but I will never go to that house! Never ever would I see the face of that lady because of whom my mother died," Lalsa answered in a raised voice.

"I will not give you even a single penny to go to London. I will disown you. You will get nothing from my property. I will never see your face again if you don't agree to come with me," Vijay went overboard. He wanted to convince Lalsa at any cost. Lalsa started crying. Vijay felt very sad looking at his daughter's situation but he had to take a strong stand for Lalsa's welfare and safety.

"I am going out of station for three days. After that I will come again to take you back. You better understand as soon as possible that there is no other option for you than to stay with the family," Vijay said sternly and left the house.

He didn't want to hurt Lalsa by threatening her or shouting at her when she really needed care and love but Lalsa's reluctance forced him to be rude with her. Vijay had become very concerned about her safety after Kanta's sudden death. He had realised the uncertainty of life which could end any moment. He didn't want Lalsa to be alone after his death.

Lalsa kept crying the whole day. In spite of Shikha's repeated requests she didn't have lunch. In the evening, when Drishtant came back, Shikha told him about everything that happened between Lalsa and her father. Drishtant went to her room with a plate of food and said, "Get up Lalsa and finish this food immediately, otherwise we will miss the movie!"

"No, Drishtant I don't want to eat anything or go anywhere."

"You know it very clearly that nobody says no to Drishtant," he said. But this time, it didn't amuse Lalsa. Tears streamed down her cheeks.

"After three days, my father will take me away, then how will you force me to do anything?" Lalsa asked with a fake smile.

"Don't worry! I will come there also!" he too faked a smile.

"But I don't want to go there, Drishtant!" Lalsa was sad but determined.

"Yes, Shikha told me. Why can't you stay here? It is like your own house. Remember, you are not alone. We all are with you in all of your decisions. Now, finish this food first and get ready immediately after that."

Drishtant still ruled over her heart and he was right that nobody could say no to him. Due to his perseverance, he was always successful in getting things done as he wished. Lalsa had a small portion of food and went for the movie with Shikha and Drishtant in spite of the turbulence in her heart. She was very tense about her future. She was absolutely sure that she didn't want to go to his father's second house but didn't know how to convince her father.

Next afternoon, Lalsa got a call from Sanya that she would reach Delhi the next morning. Lalsa told her that she was at Shikha's house, so she should come to meet her at Shikha's house. Shikha offered to send her car to pick up Sanya from the airport.

Only two days were left after which her father was supposed to take Lalsa to his second house. In spite of Shikha and her mother's efforts to assuage Lalsa, she was tense. Later in the evening, she had a low fever. When Drishtant came to her room, Lalsa was lying on the bed, she had covered her eyes with an arm. He could make out that she was crying.

"Lalsa, get up and tell me what has happened?" Drishtant asked worriedly.

"Nothing much!" Lalsa said, wiping her tears hurriedly.

"Are you worried because of your father?"

Lalsa nodded in affirmation.

"Don't worry, I will talk to him," he said confidently.

"No, Drishtant. I know him very well, he will not let me stay here anymore. He will take me to his house. I will die there!" Lalsa said helplessly and broke into tears. Drishtant sat on the bed near Lalsa and put her head on his shoulder.

"Rest assured, till I am alive, nobody can force you to do anything against your will. Do you trust me?" Drishtant asked while raising her chin with his hand and confidently looking directly into her eyes. Lalsa nodded again.

"Good! Then get ready as we are going out for dinner."

"No, please Drishtant. I have a fever. I will eat something here," Lalsa requested. Drishtant touched her forehead which was warm.

"Okay then, we will have dinner together in this room."

Shikha went to the kitchen to get dinner.

Suddenly, Lalsa's phone rang. Drishtant picked up the phone and passed it to Lalsa. It was a call from Robin. His name flashed on the screen. Lalsa looked at Drishtant with worried eyes as he had seen Robin's name on the screen before passing the phone to Lalsa. But to her surprise, Drishtant looked indifferent. There was not even a trace of anger or jealousy on his face. Lalsa thought of disconnecting the phone but then she changed her mind.

"Hello!" Lalsa said.

"Hi, Lalsa, this is Robin. My mother wants to talk to you," Robin passed the phone to his mother.

"Hi, dear! How are you?" her voice was gentle.

"I am fine, Aunty. Hope you are fine too!" Lalsa said courteously. While talking on the phone she repeatedly looked at Drishtant's face. He was busy fiddling with his phone.

"Good! Robin told me about the sudden demise of your mother and the problems you are going through. I felt very concerned about you. I can understand your situation, dear. I have called you to say that we are always there for you. You are my son's friend. He is very fond of you. I am like your mother! We can do anything for you. You can stay with us in London and we can even sponsor your education."

"Thank you, Aunty. But my father will bear all the expenses and I have a friend with whom I shall be staying in London. Thank you so much for your thoughtfulness and concern." Lalsa choked with emotion. She was touched by this gesture.

"Okay! But promise me that you will never think twice before asking me for any help!"

"Sure, Aunty! Thank you so much," Lalsa expressed her gratitude.

"Good! See you soon in London."

"Yes, Aunty!"

Robin was again on the line. "Hey, Lalsa! I am coming to Delhi day after. If you have some time, we can meet for a while."

"Sanya is also coming tomorrow morning to Delhi. Let her come, then I will let you know about the programme."

"Sure! See you soon! Good night and take care!"

"Good night!" Lalsa said and disconnected the phone. Drishtant pretended to be indifferent but Lalsa could make out that his face had turned pale. He got a shock of his life after knowing that Lalsa was planning to shift to London to pursue her studies.

"Why didn't you tell me that you are planning to go to London?" he asked.

"How could I tell you anything when I am still not sure of my future," Lalsa said sadly.

Drishtant seemed disheartened.

Shikha, Lalsa and Drishtant had their dinner and chatted till late in the night as the next day was Sunday, a holiday for Drishtant.

Next day, Sanya arrived early in the morning. Although she was a bit jet-lagged but she didn't want to waste even a single minute as she had to go to Mumbai the next day. She wanted to know all the details of Lalsa's life and everything that had happened after they had last met. Lalsa told her that Robin would also reach Delhi the next day and had requested Lalsa to meet him with Sanya to discuss the future course of action. Both of them decided to meet him the next day before Sanya's departure.

Drishtant didn't know anything about Sanya. He was amazed to see an unknown person in the house but soon he became very friendly with her. Sanya was impressed by Drishtant's looks, his courteous behaviour and concern for Lalsa.

Suddenly, Lalsa's phone rang. It was Doctor Sushant on the line.

"Hi, Lalsa! How are you? I have not heard from you since the last couple of days. Can we meet sometime today? There is some good news that I want to share with you, so where would you like to meet me?"

Lalsa got baffled as Drishtant was also standing there. But then she realised that he wasn't her boyfriend anymore. Therefore, there was no need to be scared of his reaction. She couldn't say no to Sushant, the friend and well-wisher who had stood by her side during the darkest days of her life, when even Shikha was not around.

"Doctor, I shall come to the coffee shop where we met the last time," she answered.

"Okay then, see you at 5 p.m.," he said and disconnected the phone.

Drishtant was astonished to hear that she was going to meet some doctor in a coffee shop.

"Lalsa, you are sick! Why don't you call the doctor here for your check up?"

"He isn't any regular doctor but Lalsa's friend who wants to see her," Shikha said.

"Oh I see!" Drishtant was embarrassed. "Even if he is a friend, he can always come here to see you!" he suggested. Lalsa didn't expect such a cool reaction from Drishtant. He didn't react to the phone call from Robin either. She thought that either he had changed himself or was reacting indifferently because he didn't love her anymore. She took Drishtant's suggestion and told Sushant to see her at Shikha's place as she wasn't feeling too well.

When Sushant came to see her sharp at 1 p.m., Drishtant welcomed him and took him to the drawing room. Lalsa, Shikha and Sanya joined them. He hugged Lalsa affectionately and said, "How are you dear?"

"I am fine now!" Lalsa said and introduced him to everyone. He looked dashing.

"My god, Lalsa! He is so good looking! How could you resist him?" Sanya said with a chuckle.

"Shut up!" Lalsa murmured with a smile.

Sushant was offered coffee. He chatted with everyone and then said, "Lalsa, can I talk to you alone for a while?"

"Sure!" Drishtant said and everyone left the room, leaving both of them in the drawing room.

"Lalsa, is this the same boy who broke your heart?" Sushant asked with concern.

"Yes, but how do you know?" Lalsa was curious.

"Because of the way he looks at you. His eyes light up and reflect a profound emotion for you," he said with a smile.

"No, doctor. We are just good friends now! Had he loved me, he would never have been so calm while leaving me alone with you." Lalsa said.

"Maybe, he has changed himself for you! Maybe he has understood that true love doesn't mean controlling but adjusting and respecting the individuality of the partner."

"I don't think so!" Lalsa was confused.

"Anyway, I have some good news to share with you! Resham and I are getting married to each other again."

"Oh wow! But how did it happen?" Lalsa jumped with excitement.

"Actually both of us realised that we can't live without each other," Sushant said. Lalsa was genuinely happy for him.

"Next Sunday evening, keep yourself free as we may be hosting a small party to announce our reunion. Once everything is finalised, I would love to host your friends too."

"Sure!"

Sushant paused for a while, held Lalsa's hand and said, "One more thing, Lalsa! You are very dear to me. I have a very special connection with you, maybe some past life connection. Being committed to Resham doesn't mean that I will forget you. I can do anything for you. If you ever need me in your life, just give me a call! I will immediately reach out to you in any part of the world."

He stood up to leave. Lalsa got up too. He took a couple of steps towards the door, then turned back again towards Lalsa, looked at her, hugged her, kissed her forehead and said, "Bye!" Lalsa held her tears back with a lot of self-control. She was full of gratitude for Sushant but fell completely short of words to express her emotions. With her voice choking with emotion she also said, "Bye!"

36

A Father's Demands

Next day, Lalsa's father came at 11 in the morning. Shikha, Sanya and Drishtant sat with her for emotional support while she spoke to her father.

"Bring down your stuff, Lalsa and let's go now as everybody is waiting for you at home," Vijay said. Lalsa looked at Drishtant with a pale face and helpless eyes.

Drishtant looked into her eyes and said firmly, "No, Uncle, she doesn't want to go."

"Then, where does she want to go?" Vijay asked angrily.

"She will stay here till she goes to London."

"I will not send her to London if she doesn't come with me to my house. Why should I support her financially if she doesn't care about my sentiments?" Vijay said aggressively.

Drishtant paused for a while and then said, "I will support her."

"What relationship do you share with her that you are offering to support her?"

"I am supporting her on humanitarian grounds. She is Shikha's closest friend and not less than a family member for all of us," Drishtant said firmly.

Sanya was impressed with Drishtant's firmness and confidence.

"She is not a daughter of some beggar who will live on your alms. Your support will kill her dignity and self-confidence." Vijay protested. "Listen Lalsa, if you are not coming with me then be prepared to face the consequences. I will not maintain any relation with you in future. Never come to me again. Even if I die, don't come to my funeral either." Vijay was raising his voice.

"Please calm down, Uncle!" Sanya intervened for the first time. "Uncle, she has to leave for London next month with me. Till then she can stay with me in Mumbai, and then we can leave together for London."

"No, Sanya! I want her to meet and live with her family for few days before going anywhere. If something happens to me then, my family should stand by her. She is too young, to lead her life all by herself. She would need someone to give her financial and emotional support." Vijay was determined.

Lalsa started crying. She realised that his father was right. She could not lead her life on Drishtant, Shikha or Robin's charity. Even if she wanted to shift to London, she would need a lot of money from her father. She didn't have any right to depend on anyone other than her father for her education and other expenses.

"Okay, Dad! I will come with you. Pick me up in the evening on your way back from the office. By then, I will be ready," Lalsa said sobbingly.

Vijay looked at Drishtant with stern eyes and said, "Okay, I will come in the evening!"

Vijay left after that and Lalsa went to the room with Shikha and Sanya. She wondered how her father had changed completely after her mother's death. She remembered that her father had always fulfilled all her wishes, right and wrong, even if he had to go against her mother's wishes.

She had been only nine years old and had come back from her hostel for her vacations. Her parents had taken her along to a jewellery shop to buy bangles for her mother. Lalsa liked one gold bracelet for herself, which was very heavy and big. Her mother tried to convince Lalsa as best as she could to forget about bracelet. The bracelet was too big and heavy for her to wear considering her age and size. But Lalsa was hell-bent on buying the bracelet. Her father knew that it was a sheer waste of money but his darling daughter whom he could never say no to had demanded something. In spite of her mother's strong disapproval, Vijay had bought that bracelet for her.

How could such a loving and caring father become so insensitive and callous? She wondered whether her father was really concerned about her safety. Couldn't he do anything else to save her from the impending agony? Why should she suffer because of his misdeeds and mistakes? But then he was right, she couldn't depend permanently on anyone else except her father for her expenses. She had never felt so helpless and lonely in her life.

Sanya suggested to Lalsa to meet Robin before going with her father to his house. Lalsa didn't feel like going out of the house. Shikha proposed that she could meet Robin at their place. Surprisingly, Lalsa was not scared of meeting Robin in Drishtant's presence. Her mind was numb. She felt like a person who had already lost everything in life and was no longer scared of losing anything more. Sanya called up Robin and told him to come to Shikha's house immediately. Robin reached within an hour.

37

Lalsa Faces another Dilemma

Drishtant was completely confused. He couldn't possibly let Lalsa go to her father's house against her wish. He also realised that Lalsa was going away from him forever. Instead of going to the office, he went to his room, wondering how to stop Lalsa from going away. Mentally, he was drained. His mind had stopped working. He closed his eyes to catch a nap and get refreshed. He woke up after an hour and decided to go to Shikha's room.

Surprisingly, there was no one in her room. He heard some voices from the drawing room.

When Drishtant entered the drawing room, he saw Vrinda, Shikha, Lalsa and Sanya chatting with an unknown boy. Sanya was the first to see Drishtant enter the room.

"Come Drishtant! Meet our friend Robin and Robin this is Drishtant!" Sanya introduced both of them. Robin stood up to shake hands with Drishtant who was shocked to see him in his own house. He knew that Robin had been Lalsa's first crush. He looked at Lalsa who was looking at him but immediately shifted her gaze elsewhere. Drishtant was quick to get a hold on his emotions. He shook hands with Robin smilingly.

"So guys, what have you decided?" he asked Shikha.

"Actually, Lalsa doesn't want to offend her father anymore as she is dependent on him for her financial needs. Therefore, she has decided to go with her father for a few days. After that, she will go to London with Sanya and Robin for her studies," Shikha told Drishtant.

Drishtant was too disheartened to utter a word. He felt like a loser. The person whom he loved the most was going away from him forever and he was watching it happen like a spectator. Surprisingly, he was neither angry, nor hurt after learning that Lalsa was going with Robin. He knew that he had lost Lalsa because of his own misdemeanour. He couldn't control his grief anymore.

"Please excuse me!" he said and went to his room.

After a few minutes, Vrinda came to his room and said sarcastically, "Drishtant *beta,* you had promised Lalsa that you will not let her go with her father but all your efforts were in vain. See, she is going with her father and then with Robin." Drishtant understood the underlying meaning of Vrinda's taunt.

"But Aunty, I think she trusts Robin more than me. Actually, he seems to be a nice boy. Lalsa deserves a friend like him."

"I know everything about Robin. He is a very good boy, a trustworthy and truthful friend to Lalsa but nothing more than that. Lalsa had been closer to you than to Robin. Your moral responsibility towards her is more than that of Robin. You cannot pass the buck to Robin and shrug off your responsibilities towards Lalsa."

"What to do, Vindy Aunty? I offered my support but Lalsa refused and got ready to go away. What else could I have done?"

"What else could Lalsa have opted for? She can't afford to offend her father and live on your mercy like a beggar."

"Who says she will live like a beggar? She will always be my friend."

"What about when you get married to someone? Do you think that your wife would allow you to support her? Tell me one thing honestly! Don't you love her? Would you let her go away so easily?

"No, Aunty, I think we are just friends now."

"Are you blind and senseless? Is she just a friend to you? If yes, then why did you come back from London so abruptly? Why does her pain hurt you so intensely? Why do your eyes always search for her and why does she keep waiting for you the whole day? Why don't you want her to go with her father? Why do you want her to stay here and why do you want to support her? You better understand this clearly in your heart and mind that you still love her and she also loves you, otherwise why would she trust you so much and look only towards you in times of need?"

Drishtant was stunned to listen to her logic. Gradually, she helped to clear the cloud of misunderstanding which had obscured his true feelings for Lalsa.

"If you let her go now, you will have to repent for it the rest of your life," Vrinda said.

"Don't speak like that, Aunty! I don't want her to go away at any cost but I am scared of my own self. That is the reason I am trying to hold back my feelings for her. What if I get possessive about her once again? You know, sometimes it is very difficult for me to control my anger."

"Don't be scared, Drishtant. You are a completely changed person after coming back from London. As far as your anger is concerned, there is nothing abnormal about that. It is not the anger but the completely disproportionate reaction of that anger for which we have to repent later. Therefore, the simple remedy is to not react immediately when you are angry. I have been observing that you have already mastered the trick," Vrinda said with a smile.

"Yes Aunty, you are right. The consultations I had in London really helped me to attain self-control and manage my anger better. Also the truth about my mother shared by you has helped me in eradicating my insecurity and bitterness for women from my heart."

"That's why I say that now you are completely fit to marry Lalsa," Vrinda said with a victorious smile.

"I will be very happy to marry her. But the question is, would she too be ready to accept me?" Drishtant's eyes twinkled.

"I think you should ask her yourself."

"No, I am scared to do that. You talk to her first and get her consent. After that, I will talk to her."

"Okay!" Vrinda said happily and left the room to talk to Lalsa. Drishtant felt as if he was flying. He was extremely happy and anxious to talk to Lalsa in the hope that she also felt the same way.

Robin had left by then. When Vrinda entered the room, Lalsa was packing her clothes.

"So finally you have decided to go?" Vrinda asked.

"Yes, Aunty, I will have to go. My father was right. How can I stay here? I have already bothered you a lot. I don't have any right to stay here anymore," Lalsa answered with teary eyes.

"Don't be crazy! You are as dear to me as Shikha is. You have the full right to stay here as long as you want," Vrinda paused for a moment and said, "Lalsa, I want to ask you something very important. If I say Drishtant loves you and wants to marry you, would you give him a second chance?"

Lalsa was bewildered. It took her some time to gather herself. "But Aunty, you know how our relationship has failed in the past. We can be good friends but not a happy couple," she said.

"Lalsa didn't you notice that Drishtant is a changed person now? He is calm, peaceful and balanced. Trust me, I would never ask you to marry him just because of your circumstances. I know Drishtant was a difficult person to be with but it is human to make mistakes. All of us are flawed in different ways but that does not mean we don't deserve second chances. I know, it is not easy to accommodate all the mistakes but you can meet each other halfway and respect your partner's perspective also.

"But Aunty, you know Drishtant would never adjust even a bit. Is it only a woman's responsibility to adjust?"

"No, it is not. Both the partners have to look out for each other. In your case, both of you were very young and immature, and none of you was ready to adjust. According to your perspective, whatever he did was wrong while your actions were wrong according to his perspective. Remember, if you suffered in his love, he also suffered in your love. You suffered because of his possessiveness but he too suffered because of your perspective and preferences that were very different from his."

Lalsa had never thought that unknowingly and unintentionally she had also hurt Drishtant. Vrinda continued, "You are the only girl whom he has loved in his entire life. In spite of many distractions in London, he never cheated on you. In the past, he wanted to change you but now he wants to change himself for you and has already started making an effort in that direction. So please accept him now as acceptance is the greatest virtue of love. Lalsa beta, true love is hard to find, so don't let him go out of your life.

"What if he misbehaves with me again?"

"What lies ahead cannot be seen but what exists right now is evident. He loves you and you love him too. He has changed himself for you, and he is still willing to walk the extra mile. Therefore, it is worth giving a second chance to your relationship. Take the plunge and cherish each other," Vrinda advised.

"Aunty, I am not sure whether we should get married or not."

"Before making any decision, be sure in your mind about whether you love him or not. If you don't love him, then you should not live with him even for a single day. If you are confident that you still love him, then you have two choices, either shun him forever and live with bitter memories of your past or forgive him and move forward happily by making this relationship work," Sanya intervened in the middle of their conversation.

"I completely agree with Sanya. I would advise you as a mother that if you still love him, then please give him a chance. Believe me, he really deserves a second chance."

"Aunty, there wasn't even a single day when I didn't miss him. I shall never be able to love anyone else the way I have loved him. But what about him? He never said that he still loves me," Lalsa said softly. She seemed to be convinced with everything Vrinda said.

"I am going to send him to your room. He himself will tell you how he feels about you," Vrinda said with a smile. She kissed Lalsa on the forehead and left the room. Sanya hugged Lalsa with excitement and happiness and left the room along with Shikha. After a few minutes, when Drishtant entered the room, he saw Lalsa engrossed with settling her clothes in the bag.

"Once again you are planning to go away from me, Lalsa?"

"What else can I do, Drishtant," Lalsa said sadly.

"Please don't go, Lalsa. You are the love of my life. You are the only one in my lonely life whom I have ever loved and will love till eternity! Please don't leave me alone. I will not be able to live without you! Please marry me!" Drishtant held her arm and confessed. The clothes which Lalsa was folding to put in her bag fell from her hands. She was taken aback with the sudden revelation made by Drishant of his love for her.

"What? What did you say?"

"I Iove you, darling and I want to marry you."

Lalsa paused for a while, then gently freed her arm from his hand and said, "No, I can't believe that. After our break-up, you didn't call me even once! How do I believe that you still love me? You just want to help me out of sympathy."

"You are a fool! I called you so many times and each time I told you only one thing that I love you. Why do you think I came back to India without completing my course in London? When Shikha told me about your condition, I left everything and came running to you. And you are planning to run away from me forever to London. Do you want more proof?"

"Was that you who whispered, 'I love you!' on the phone?" Lalsa was thrilled.

"Of course! Who else but I could dare to say these three words to you?" Drishtant said with a loud laughter.

Suddenly, Lalsa's face shone with joy. She never knew that everything would happen so fast. Drishtant hugged her and said, "I love you and only you in this entire world."

"But what about my studies? I want to be a fashion designer and launch my own line of couture. It would not be possible after marriage," Lalsa seemed concerned.

"Who told you that you can't pursue your studies and career after marriage? If you want to go to London, we will go together to pursue our education. After completing your course, you will have my full support to make your dreams come true. Trust me, your happiness is the prime concern of my life," Drishtant said with a peck on her forehead.

Lalsa never knew that God had this plan for her and there was light at the end of the tunnel.

38

How to Move Forward

Drishtant called Shikha, Vrinda and Sanya. All were overwhelmed to know that they wanted to live together.

"But how to move forward is a big question because if we tell Lalsa's father that both of you want get married, he would be happy but may not allow Lalsa to stay in the same house. He would take Lalsa away till the marriage but Lalsa doesn't want to go to that house at all," Sanya expressed her concern.

"Yes, you are right, Sanya. There is one more problem. Less than a month ago, her mother died and according to Punjabi rituals, her formal marriage function may not be possible before eleven months," Vrinda made a revelation.

"I think, they should go for an immediate simple marriage in the temple and inform the elders afterwards," Shikha came up with a suggestion.

Everyone agreed to that as they didn't want to take any chances. All the cousins were informed to join and witness the marriage with the vow to keep it a secret. 4 p.m. was the auspicious time for their marriage to be solemnised according to the pandit *ji*. Meanwhile, Shikha and her mother bought the wedding clothes and other important things like *chuda*, *kaleere, sindoor* and *mehendi* for Lalsa. Sanya and Shikha helped Lalsa in getting ready.

Drishtant also bought his clothes. His cousins went to the temple to make all the arrangements. Everyone was very excited. Actually, it was a thrilling experience for all the youngsters to arrange this secret wedding without informing the elders. Sanya told everything to Robin and invited him to witness the wedding at the temple. Robin was a bit taken aback at the sudden development of Lalsa's marriage. He had truly loved Lalsa and had always dreamt of marrying her. But he knew that under the changed circumstances, Lalsa would be more comfortable and happy with Drishtant as she had shared a very intense relationship with him. He was happy to see Lalsa with the person she truly loved. Finally, he decided to attend their wedding.

Lalsa invited Doctor Sushant and Resham also. They were super excited to join them.

Drishtant's father was astounded to know that his son was getting married. Being a simple person, he accepted their marriage immediately and became a part of their happiness.

Shikha's mother called her husband also because a married couple was needed to perform *kanyadaan*. Shikha's father and mother performed *kanyadaan* ceremony. The whole ceremony ended at 6 p.m. In the middle of the wedding rituals, Robin also arrived. He witnessed the marriage with a smile. He was genuinely happy for Lalsa. After the wedding, he wished both good luck and left for the airport. Lalsa and Drishtant promised to see him soon in London.

Everyone else headed to Drishtant's house.

Lalsa's father came at 8 p.m. to take her back. He sat in the drawing room waiting for Lalsa to come. He was amazed to see the hustle-bustle in the house. Suddenly, Vrinda entered the drawing room with a box of sweets in her hand.

"Namaskar, *bhai sahib*! Please have some sweets!" she said with a broad smile and offered sweets to him.

Vijay took a piece of the sweet. "Is there any occasion today in your house?" he asked inquisitively.

"Yes, *bhai sahib*! Drishtant got married today!"

"Oh, I see!" answered Vijay.

"Can you please call, Lalsa. I am getting late."

"How can she go with you, *bhai sahib*?" Vrinda said laughingly.

"Why? Why can't she go with me?" Vijay was getting irritated by her weird behaviour.

"I just told you Drishtant got married today, so how can she go?" Vrinda said.

"Why? How is she concerned with his marriage?" Vijay said irritatingly.

"Come on *bhai sahib*! She is his wife. Who else can be more concerned than her?" Vijay was stunned for a while. He thought that he had not heard her properly.

"What did you say? I didn't get it!" Vijay was completely confused.

"You have heard it right, *bhai sahib*! Lalsa is now Drishtant's wife. A few hours back, they tied the knot in the temple."

The expression on Vijay's face changed completely. He was baffled. But after a while, when he finally realised what had happened, his face turned soft and his eyes were full of tears.

"Can you please call her?" Vijay's throat was choked with emotion.

Drishtant accompanied Lalsa to the drawing room. She was dressed in a red bridal dress and looked beautiful. Both of them touched his feet. Lalsa looked towards her father. Vijay couldn't control his emotions anymore. He hugged Lalsa and started crying. Shikha brought water for him. He had water and sat on the chair near Lalsa.

"I had so many dreams for your marriage but I didn't know that I would miss the opportunity to witness the occasion. I know it was my fault. I want to thank Drishtant and the whole family for accepting my daughter. I couldn't do anything for her happiness but all of you accepted her as your own family member and gave her the happiness that she rightly deserved. I feel honoured to have a son-in-law like Drishtant. I am indebted to you for the rest of my life." Vijay said with teary eyes. Then he placed his hand on Lalsa's head and said, "Lalsa, over the years, your mother collected a lot of stuff for your marriage. I will bring everything tomorrow."

"There is no need for anything, Uncle!" said Drishtant.

"No, it is her blessings, so please don't say no!"

"Okay, Uncle!" Drishtant said humbly.

Vijay stayed for dinner because of Vrinda's insistence. He was clearly very emotional and tears constantly filled his eyes. While going back he held Drishtant's hands in both his hands and said, "Thanks, son! Thank you for taking this decision. Kanta and I looked after Lalsa like a princess. But after her mother's death, she became very lonely. Now that she has finally found happiness in your companionship, please take care of my daughter and don't let her miss us," Vijay said with tearful eyes. Then he thanked Drishtant's father, Shikha's parents and all the family members. There was a strange peace and serenity on his face. After he hugged Lalsa, he left the house.

Next day in the afternoon, when Lalsa and Drishtant were in their bedroom, the house help knocked on the door and informed that Lalsa's father had come to see them.

Both of them went to the drawing room.

Vijay hugged Lalsa. It seemed as though he could cry any time.

"Lalsa, I have brought all the stuff that you may need your clothes, bed covers, cutlery and a number of other things which your mother had collected over a long period of time for you. Wherever she went, she kept collecting various things to gift you at the time of your wedding. She had collected a lot of jewellery that she didn't even tell you about. I have brought everything here. She had a life insurance of one crore and you are the beneficiary of that. I am also giving you the papers of the house in which we lived with your mother. You do whatever you want to do with that house. Then he took out few packets containing money for all the family members with their names on the envelopes and a beautiful watch and a cheque of a certain amount for Drishtant.

"This is too much, Uncle! Please don't do this!" said Drishtant.

Vijay folded his hands and said, "Please accept these small gifts. Everything that you all have done for my daughter can never be reciprocated. This is just a small gesture to say thank you, so please accept it."

Drishtant and Lalsa could not say anything.

"Lalsa, can I talk to you for a while?" Vijay asked hesitantly.

"Yes, sure!" Lalsa said and everybody left the room, leaving both of them behind. Vijay put his hand on Lalsa's head and said, "Lalsa, my daughter you were and you will always be my princess. Just remember, your father can do anything for you. Therefore, never hesitate to ask for anything. If you don't want to come to my house, it is fine. I understand your sentiments. Earlier, I insisted you come to that house because I was worried about your safety. I didn't want you to be alone in case anything happened to me. Now, the circumstances are different. You have Drishtant and his whole family behind you. I will not force you to come to my second house now. I will come to see you or we can meet anywhere at a place of your choice. But now, with folded hands I request you to please forgive me for my past deeds," Vijay started crying, even Lalsa could not hold her tears.

With a lump in his throat, Vijay continued, "One more thing which I want to say is that your husband is an angel who has married you in such miserable circumstances. Therefore, try to keep him, his family, and most importantly yourself happy."

Vijay broke down again. Lalsa gave him a glass of water. After sipping water, Vijay said, "Lalsa, if you want that your husband should always love you, then always respect him and his family. Now this is your family, they have stood by you in the darkest phase of your life, so value their kindness. Give them back the same love and respect.

"Okay, Dad!" said Lalsa. After a long time, she was feeling sad for her father.

"Promise me, that you will call me every day and once you are back from London, you will meet me at least once a week," Vijay said with a smile.

Lalsa also smiled and said, "Okay Dad, I promise and you take care of yourself!"

After Vijay left, Vrinda entered the room. She sat near Lalsa, held her hand and said, "Lalsa, I have performed all the rites of your *kanyadaan*, so nowI am your mother, and I want you to make a promise to me."

"Please tell me Aunty, what I can do? I am already indebted to you. I will do whatever you say," Lalsa hugged Vrinda affectionately.

"Lalsa, I am the one who convinced both of you to marry each other, so I want you to always be happy. Everything seems fine now but nobody has seen the future. I have seen many people change in marriages. Their love vanishes and eventually they separate from each other. In that case, most of the time, women have to suffer more because of their financial dependence on their husbands. Although, I am sure Drishtant will never change but even then, I would like you to be economically independent for your own self-esteem and security, so that in future you don't have to compromise just because of your financial insecurity. Promise me that you will give your hundred per cent to your education and career along with strengthening your relationship with Drishtant. When you come back from London, I want to see you as a happy wife and the winner who excels in her career."

"Sure, Aunty! Going through such a tough time at such a young age has really taught me a lot. But I promise you that I will emerge stronger and wiser. I also agree with you that for any girl, being financially independent is even more important than getting married. I have seen my cousin Neha *didi* compromise with her husband's infidelity and have heard about so many other women suffering just because of their financial dependence on their husbands. Believe me,

Aunty, I will take both, my career and my marriage, very seriously and do my best to succeed as a professional and as a wife. I promise to make you feel proud of me with your blessings," Lalsa got up with her revived confidence and determination to embark on a new journey of her life with a resolution to win the world.

Acknowledgements

The characters in this book are inspired by what I see around me, and I would like to thank those who helped me to weave this story:

My daughter, Vaishali Rai, the inspiration behind this book;

My son, Puneet Rai;

My friends Anju Khera, Alka Dasoar and Vineeta Khanna who shared interesting stories with me;

My son, Himanshu Rai;

My friend Shashi Khurana;

My editor Simran Kaur for her inputs;

And Ajay Mago, Publisher, Om Books International, for liking the story.

Hope you enjoy reading it!